THE BRUNELLI
BABY BARGAIN

THE BRUNELLI
BABY BARGAIN

BY

KIM LAWRENCE

First published in Great Britain 2009
Large Print edition 2009
Harlequin Mills & Boon Limited,
Eton House, 18-24 Paradise Road,
Richmond, Surrey TW9 1SR

© Kim Lawrence 2009

ISBN: 978 0 263 20612 8

Set in Times Roman 16½ on 18½ pt.
16-0809-49158

Harlequin Mills & Boon policy is to use papers that are
natural, renewable and recyclable products and made
from wood grown in sustainable forests. The logging and
manufacturing process conform to the legal environmental
regulations of the country of origin.

Printed and bound in Great Britain
by CPI Antony Rowe, Chippenham, Wiltshire

CHAPTER ONE

SAM took a deep sustaining breath and muttered, 'Don't bottle it now,' to herself as she approached the young woman who sat behind a large glass desk. With her blonde hair and hourglass figure the woman had the kind of beauty that always attracted men's attention.

Diminutive redheads with freckles, on the other hand, were not so universally lusted after, at least in Sam's experience, although it had seemed for a while that Will had thought differently—until the day she had walked in and found her erstwhile fiancé in bed with a beautiful blonde.

Normally when Sam's thoughts touched on this memorable occasion she experienced a wave of nausea that turned her sensitive stomach inside out, but not this time. This time her stomach was already paralysed with sheer terror.

Her eyelashes brushed her cheeks as she squeezed her eyes closed and took a second breath, willing her frantically racing heart, which felt as though it were imminently about to break through her ribcage, to slow. She forced a smile; if a person acted as though they expected to be shown the door, they probably would be.

She had taken several hours to achieve the appearance of someone who might consider strolling into the headquarters of a multinational empire and demanding to see the man who was top of the food chain as something she did every day of the week, but, catching sight of her reflection in a mirrored panel on the opposite wall, she knew her efforts had been wasted.

This was not going to work.

Ignoring the voice of pessimism, or rather reality, in her head, Sam pinned the smile back on and cleared her throat. The sound attracted the attention of the receptionist, but only briefly because at that exact moment the glass lift doors to Sam's left silently opened to reveal another blonde, a tall voluptuous one wearing a very small red dress.

The girl behind the desk stared and so did Sam; so also did the men with cameras who had appeared from nowhere as if by magic.

The ravishing blonde seemed totally unfazed by the flash photography and the volley of questions the paparazzi flung in her direction. She simply bared her perfect teeth in a brilliant smile and proved that, even though she had made the transition from modelling to Hollywood, she still knew how to strut her stuff. Flanked by two large muscular bodyguards, she glided through the foyer pausing once or twice to give the hungry press a pose while responding with an enigmatic smile and a coy, 'No comment,' to their demands to know if she and Cesare were back together.

As the door closed leaving only the heavy scent of the actress's exotic perfume in the air Sam was wondering much the same thing—talk about bad timing! The last thing any man wanted to hear was the news she had come to deliver, but she imagined that this was doubly true of a man who had just been reconciled with the love of his life.

Sam sighed and tried to push the image of the actress from her head; she wasn't here to compete for the Italian's attention or his affections. She wasn't even slightly interested in Cesare Brunelli's love life and she had no wish to be part of it, something she would make quite clear.

Her only reason for being here was simple: tell him and leave. The ball would then be in his court and if he decided not to pick it up then that would make life a lot simpler.

All she had to do was tell him.

It was now or never!

At the moment never was looking pretty damn good!

She winced as her designer shoes pinched. They had been a bargain, but were also a painful half a size too small, though the confidence boost they gave her far outweighed any discomfort.

'I'm…' She stopped as she tried to introduce herself to the woman behind the desk, her mouth open, her confident manner wobbling into pessimistic anxiety.

What was she meant to say?

I'm Sam, but that won't mean anything—your boss doesn't know my name, he doesn't even know the colour of my eyes, he's oblivious to the fact I have freckles, and my hair is ginger. But I thought that given the circumstances it was only polite to let him know my news face to face as opposed to some more impersonal method—I'm having his baby.

As she stood in the reception of Cesare's offices, Sam thought of the differences between an Italian billionaire and a girl who juggled her finances each month. She had probably earned less during her entire working life than Cesare did in a minute! Still, things were improving professionally—she'd put in four years of un-glamorous work on the local newspaper in the Scottish market town where she had been born, making tea before rising to cover the weddings and church fêtes. Now, finally, her hard work had paid dividends and she had landed a job, although a very junior one, admittedly, at a national daily here in London.

'Yeah, things are better than they were in my day,' the established older female journalist who had taken her under her wing had told her. 'You have talent, Sam,' she conceded, making Sam glow with pride.

'But,' she warned, 'you need to give one hundred per cent if you want people to think you are serious and, while scruples aren't a *bad* thing exactly, you need to be a bit more... flexible. Oh, and it goes without saying that the last thing you want at this point in your career is a high-maintenance relationship.' At this point she had laughed and Sam had joined in. 'Or a family...professional suicide!'

Baby!

Sam wasn't laughing now as she considered this new and frankly scary detour in her hitherto predictable life. She had been scared—she still was—but there had never been any tortured soul-searching; it had simply never occurred to her not to have this baby.

Underneath the scariness and the panic there was a deep-seated and totally inexplicable feeling of *rightness*... This was not a feeling she anticipated the father of her accidental baby would share. But just because he wouldn't want anything to do with the baby didn't mean he didn't have the right to know.

Sam had steeled herself for his inevitable anger

and suspicion that she had told herself would be normal for any man in such circumstances. What was less normal was the strange sense of inner serenity she had tapped into—a serenity she hadn't known she possessed, although she also wondered whether it might just be a symptom of delayed shock.

A shaky sigh left her lungs as Sam shook her head. She had only had a fortnight to get used to the idea and it still hadn't fully sunk in yet—in fact the whole situation had a surreal quality.

Her hand went to her belly, still flat under her jacket and her lips curved into a wry smile. No doubt the idea would start to feel more real when her waistline began to expand.

She addressed the girl behind the desk once more. 'I'm…Samantha Muir and…'

The girl looking slightly bored now the actress and her noisy entourage had left, lifted the phone she was speaking into away from her ear and, without making eye contact with Sam, said, 'First left.'

Sam blinked. This was not the way any of her mental versions of this scene had played.

The shoes must really have worked!

The shoes in question were at that moment nailed to the floor. She couldn't move, she was so shocked at not even having her identity queried or the reason for her visit questioned.

'First left?' she echoed, inwardly wondering why she was still standing there. The woman wanted her to go through that door, she wasn't to know Sam didn't have an appointment so she shouldn't under any circumstances volunteer the information.

What was holding her back? Those inconvenient scruples, that awful compulsion to tell the truth in moments when a white lie or silence worked much better, or simply gutless fear?

With a hint of impatience the receptionist nodded and waved long red-painted nails in the direction of the door before turning her attention back to the phone.

This is too easy, persisted the voice of suspicion in Sam's head.

'Easy is good,' Sam retorted under her breath. If this was a case of crossed wires it was working to her advantage so she'd be a dope not to go with the flow. She lifted her chin and once again fixed a confident smile on her pale face—she was tapping into previously unexpected acting talents—and walked through the door without knocking.

It was a bit of an anticlimax, as the room she found herself in was not large. The only furniture was a small desk in one corner and some easy chairs set along one wall. A door beside the desk opened and a slim thirty-something man with thinning sandy hair and a harassed manner walked in, then dropped the file of papers he was holding when he saw her.

'You're a woman.'

Under normal circumstances Sam would have responded to this accusation, because it was definitely an accusation, with ironic humour. But humour and irony were both beyond her at the moment.

Instead she nodded cautiously and said, 'Hello, I'm Sam Muir and I'd like—'

'*Sam!*' He slapped a hand to his forehead and groaned. 'That explains it, of course. And just when I thought that this day couldn't get any worse.'

Sam, feeling increasingly bewildered, gave another vague nod. 'I'm here to see Mr Brunelli…?'

As she spoke her mental barrier slipped and a dark image flickered across her retina. The blurry lines solidified into features until she could see each strongly sculpted line and individual angle of Cesare Brunelli's face.

It seemed amazing now that she had had no precognition of danger the first time she had looked into the face of the tall man who had towered over her.

The impact of his beauty had been like a physical blow drawing the breath from her burning lungs like the heat from a furnace being drawn into a vacuum.

She had been dimly conscious of emotions deep inside her stirring, breaking free of self-imposed restraints, but had felt strangely disconnected from what had been happening to her. Her innate ability to distance herself emotionally and analyse what she was doing and why had deserted her totally. Of course she hadn't recognised this until it had been too late—the damage had been done!

When she had been with him she hadn't been able to control her pounding heartbeat, the weakness in her shaking limbs or the burning heat that had washed over her skin.

It wasn't just the stern symmetry and powerful planes of his bronzed patrician features, or the curve of his mouth, it was no individual feature but the combination that made him so beautiful.

Even now, twelve weeks later, the memory of his face made Sam's throat ache, but now she could think about her reaction and what had happened later more objectively.

She could not deny he was a good-looking man who possessed an arrogant sexuality she was not totally immune to, but what had happened had been the result of a freak set of circumstances rather than anything more momentous.

He would probably turn out to be quite ordinary, she thought. She'd probably just built him up in her mind into something extraordinary to defend her own behaviour because nothing short of a rampant, irresistible sex god could be responsible for her fall from grace. She was looking for excuses.

Whereas the plain truth was there were no

excuses; she'd been reckless and stupid. She'd had a moment of weakness—actually an entire night of weakness, but this was something she chose not to dwell on—and now she had to live with it.

She would probably see him and discover he bore no resemblance to her romanticised image of a brooding, damaged hero in need of comfort that only she could give.

Quickly she shied away from the subject of *giving* and turned her thoughts instead to the present. Dragging her attention back to the sandy-haired young man, she noticed he was rifling through some papers he now had in his hand.

'This might be a problem… It looks like your CV has gone walkabout too, my God!' he exclaimed in disgust. 'That woman really was a total liability!' He put aside the papers and glanced up at Sam, adding as an apologetic afterthought, 'Sorry, it's not your fault.'

Actually it was.

A fresh wave of disgust and shame washed over Sam.

Who else was there to blame? She'd kissed Cesare first, kissed a total stranger.

The memory of him was indelibly stamped into her consciousness—the way his face had been illuminated by the sudden flash of white lightning outside the window, and the way things had twisted painfully in her chest when she had seen the terrible bleakness that had shone deep in his incredible eyes and the utter frustration stamped on his dark features.

Unable to voice the words of comfort, unable to force any sound besides a choking sigh past the emotional congestion in her throat, she had instead reached out and taken his face between her hands.

The actions had been spontaneous, and, she had realised almost immediately, a mistake. He had stiffened at the touch of her mouth, his own lips remaining unresponsive under the pressure of hers.

Kissing a gorgeous man who didn't want to be kissed might be something that any number of women her age could laugh off with a shrug, but Sam did not possess that skill.

She hadn't wanted to laugh; she'd wanted to die from sheer mortification. She had started to lift her head, started to mutter a mortified apology, and would have removed her hands had his own fingers not come up to cover hers and hold them against his face.

Sam's heart thudded again as she remembered his fingers tangling in hers, the fine muscles along his jaw tensing, his nostrils flaring as he slurred something thick in his own language.

She had felt rather than heard the groan that had seemed to be dragged from deep inside him before being lost in her mouth.

She had started it!

It was absolutely no excuse that he had looked as if he needed kissing.

Of course, if he hadn't kissed her back and the storm hadn't knocked out the electricity…there would have been no problem. No problem, no scalding shame and no baby!

She bit down hard on her lip and subdued the images that rose shameful and graphic in her head… It had happened and it was pretty pointless given the consequences in pretending it hadn't, but nothing could be achieved by endless post-mortems.

Tension drawing the soft lines of her pale face taut, her hand went unconsciously to her stomach. He would not want to know, which suited her fine. She could walk out of the door knowing that she had done the right thing.

'Is Mr Brunelli actually here?' she asked. Half of her wanted the answer to be negative.

The man sighed, his glance swivelling significantly towards the door behind him before he nodded and belatedly introduced himself. 'I'm Tim Andrews. Call me Tim,' he added with an easy-going smile.

After a hesitation Sam took the hand he extended, her gaze sliding to the door. If she moved quickly she could be through it before this nice man could stop her.

'You're shaking,' the man said suddenly, concern replacing the harassed expression on his face as Sam pulled her hand away.

She thrust her hands in the pockets of her jacket and told herself to relax. What was the worst they could do? To be forcibly ejected by Security would be a new experience. Although her last new experience had not turned out so well, however blissfully perfect it had been at the time.

'I've come a long way to see Mr Brunelli.' It

had actually just been a couple of Tube rides, but she saw no harm in exaggeration given the circumstances. 'And I'm not leaving until I do. I mean it.' Sam wished she felt half as resolved as she sounded.

There was a startled pause before Tim said, 'I believe you.'

I wish I did, she thought.

'I'll do what I can but…' He gave a shrug that told her to be prepared to be disappointed. 'Would you like to take a seat?'

Sam, who would have quite liked to be somewhere else—anywhere else—walked to one of the chairs set against the wall and sat down.

After a tap on the dividing door Tim Andrews walked through.

From where she was sitting Sam could hear the sound of raised voices, or at least one anyway, and that was the only one she was hearing. It brought it all back with a rush, or would have if she had not sternly pushed it away, which wasn't easy when the owner of the deep, gravelly, accented tone was standing on the other side of that wall.

Perhaps she'd been wrong to opt for the personal touch—a letter or an email, in fact anything that did not bring her into physical contact with this man, might have been better.

It wasn't as if she had anything to prove to anyone else or herself.

Sam wasn't conscious of getting to her feet or crossing the room, but she must have because the next thing she knew she was standing in the open doorway.

The room beyond was vast, but Sam was oblivious to the oak panelling and wall of glass that framed a view of the river. Her glance only skimmed the eclectic mix of modern designer and antique furniture before going straight to the tall, lean, broad-shouldered figure standing with his back to her.

He turned his head slightly, revealing the high, intelligent forehead, strong line of an aquiline nose and the slightly squared angle of a firm shaven jaw.

The man she had spent the night with had worn his hair collar-length and his jaw had been covered in stubble. He had been raw and earthy, as elemental as the storm that had raged outside as they had made love.

This man had a smooth jaw line and his hair was cut close to his head. Casual and crumpled jeans had been replaced by a beautifully tailored grey suit that shrieked designer. He looked the epitome of masculine elegance and sophistication.

Suddenly this didn't feel like a polite formality— it felt like a major mistake. Sam was gripped by an urgent and primitive compulsion to turn and run, and she would have obeyed this instinct if her legs or for that matter any other parts of her body, had shown any inclination to follow instructions.

'Shall I shut the door? She's out there and—'

'No, leave it open. Candice does not understand the concept of less is more when it comes to perfume.'

As Sam saw Cesare's aristocratic nose wrinkle in distaste she wondered if this display was less to do with genuine repugnance to the exotic scent and more to do with the person it reminded him of.

Did it just bring memories of his time with Candice flooding back or fill him with helpless longing?

Neither possibility made Sam feel particularly cheerful. Ever since she'd read a newspaper article on Cesare's relationship with Candice, Sam had been wondering if it had been the beautiful actress's face he had been seeing in his head when he had made love to her. For all Sam knew those liquid Italian endearments that had melted her might have been intended for someone quite different, someone who really was his *bella mia*, his beautiful blonde ex-fiancée—except—now the *ex* part was in question.

'Look, I'm sorry about Candice but she—'

'There is no need to explain Candice to me, Tim—she is sensationally single minded when she decides on something. I take it the news of her presence here was leaked?'

The slighter man responded to this dry enquiry with a rueful grimace. 'I'm afraid so.'

'She was never one to waste a good photo opportunity.'

'About this girl, Cesare, she's travelled to get here—couldn't you just see her? You don't have to actually give her the job.'

As Sam listened she finally understood the reason for the open doors that she had so far encountered—they thought she was an applicant for a job!

This realisation might have made her laugh if it had not been for the fact that the only thing Sam was really conscious of at that moment was the man who responded to this coaxing comment from Tim with a contemptuous snort.

Just her luck it turned out Cesare actually was a rampant sex god!

'I was quite specific I do not want a female PA.'

'Well, the agency couldn't *say* that, could they? Not without being accused of sexual discrimination.'

'So this is why a woman was included in the shortlist? To pay lip service to equality?'

She watched as Cesare Brunelli walked around the desk, his face set in lines of irritation, then without taking his eyes from the other man he picked up a smooth green rock shot through with iridescent streaks of gold and began to rub it between his palms.

Sam, her eyes glued to his long brown fingers, ran a tongue over her dry lips as her stomach filled with a flock of butterflies at the thought of those fingers on her skin, the skilful touch leaving trails of fire.

'Is that the same stone you brought back from the peak when we did that Himalaya trek?'

'Yes.' As he let the stone settle in the palm of one hand Cesare's expression was unreadable.

It was no struggle for Sam to see him clinging to some sheer cliff face. He looked like a man who liked to push the boundaries and himself.

'That was some experience, wasn't it?' Tim enthused, a grin spreading across his face. 'Even if I didn't make it to the top,' he added ruefully. 'But next time I'm not going to chicken out. I'm going to keep up with the big boys. Then I'll see the view for myself.'

The sound of the stone being set back down on the desk brought the sandy-haired Englishman's eyes to the tall Italian's face.

'But I will not.'

The moment the words were out of his mouth

Cesare regretted them. He disliked self-pity in others and even more so in himself.

Colour flooded Tim's face. 'I'm really sorry. I can't seem to open my mouth without—'

'Saying something to remind me that I'm blind? The fact you forget it is why I keep you around. That and the fact your schoolboyish looks lull the opposition into a false sense of security. You're about the only person who doesn't walk on eggshells around me.'

There had been one other.

Cesare closed his eyes, but it did not stop him hearing her voice in his head. Sometimes he thought she had been an erotic figment of his imagination, but his imagination would not have been capable of conjuring such vivid memories. He heard her voice saying things that nobody else had dared, but every word and every accusation had been true.

'Gutless wonder' had perhaps been a little harsh, but a flicker of a smile crossed his face at the recollection—his response at the time of her comments had not been such a tolerant or objective one.

She had become the innocent—though provocative—focus of all the inner rage and impotent fury that consumed him.

His nerve endings had been exposed and stripped bare—perhaps just by her voice. The husky quality certainly had the ability to dig its way under a man's skin.

She had said things that nobody else would, things that had needed saying. She had ripped away his defences with a few observations and made him feel what he had been trying not to—pain!

She had tapped into the protective hollowness that he had been carrying around.

The sex had been something else—a mistake, but the sort that he would like to make again, he mused, a reflective smile playing around the corners of his lips.

'People always walk on eggshells around you,' Tim retorted, snapping Cesare out of his reverie, 'because you intimidate the hell out of them.' That much at least had not changed since the accident.

'You're suggesting I'm not a fair man? That I'm a bully?' Cesare asked, sounding interested rather than offended by the possibility.

'I'm suggesting you're a man who sets himself high standards and expects others to live up to them, but not everyone has your—focus.'

It had taken more than mere focus for Cesare to overcome the personal demons that had arisen after he'd suffered losing his sight.

It had taken a will of steel.

'About this girl…?'

Cesare's fingers drilled an impatient tattoo on the desk. 'You know my opinion of this sort of pointless political correctness, so why waste this woman's time and mine?'

'She was included by mistake, her name is Sam…' Tim's explanation trailed away as he added coaxingly, 'Couldn't you just see her?' The moment the words left his lips a flush mounted his fair, freckled face and he broke off before saying awkwardly, 'I mean…'

Cesare lifted a sardonic brow. 'I know what you *mean*, Timothy,' he said, amusement in his voice. 'And I do wish you would stop trying so hard to spare my feelings. But, no, I will not…*see* her. I can hardly be accused of sexual discrimination towards women in the workplace.

Is it not a fact that we employ more women in senior management positions than any other comparable company?'

'Yes…'

'I have no problem with women in the workplace—it is just a woman in my office I do not want.' He found the idea of having unseen eyes filled with pity following him around the office intolerable.

'This one might be different.'

'You mean she might not be caring and compassionate and she might not be unable to perform incidental tasks like sorting my diary because she is so busy oozing empathy and protecting me. It didn't matter how rude I was—'

'And you were.'

'It didn't matter.'

'She still fell in love with you! I should have your problem,' Tim muttered.

A spasm of distaste contorted Cesare's dark lean features as he snorted. 'Please do not confuse that sort of soppy sentimentality with love.'

CHAPTER TWO

'I WON'T fall in love with you.' Sam felt pretty safe in making this statement, though obviously she wouldn't have felt as comfortable if she had been discussing falling in lust.

She had fallen deep and desperately in lust with this man about ten seconds after she'd set eyes on him. Lust had made her principles and self-respect vanish in a hot flash of indiscriminating hormones...

But love was a very different kind of beast; love bore no resemblance to a bolt of lightning that robbed you of your ability to think; love wasn't about chemicals; it happened gradually, it grew in strength and it endured.

Lust, on the other hand, was made of much more flimsy material. It had no staying power...which was why Sam could look at

Cesare now and feel nothing but…oh, God, looking at him was not a good idea!

The sound of her voice made both men turn their heads in her direction and Sam was forced to rapidly re-evaluate the staying power of her lust.

The hormones were still there and active!

She knew Cesare couldn't see her but it felt as though he were staring right at her.

Sam's heart was pumping so fast she could hardly drag air into her lungs.

Cesare looked so different. Would he shrug off the veneer of cultured sophistication as easily as he might shrug that impeccably tailored jacket over his broad shoulders…?

Well, she wasn't going to hang around to find out, Sam reminded herself as the image of Cesare in her head began to shed more than his jacket!

'I'm not here about the job, Mr Brunelli.' And she wasn't here to lust after his body. Lusting was what had got her in this mess to begin with!

His incredible eyes, sloe-dark and framed by preposterously long, curling ebony lashes, were trained directly on her face. Sam felt as if that piercing stare were seeing, not just her face, but the thoughts in her head, and as these thoughts involved him wearing very little it was a deeply disturbing feeling.

Cesare stilled, his hands clenching into fists at his sides as the deep little voice with the unique husky resonance hit him like a slap in the face.

He'd searched for her and been unable to find her, the woman who had appeared in his life then quietly vanished leaving only the scent of her body on his bed sheets to show she had not been a dream.

She was here. *She* had found *him*. A slow smile curved his lips as anticipation uncurled in his belly. After the accident his sexual appetite had gone into hibernation, but had been re-awoken with a vengeance by the owner of this voice. When she had vanished so, inexplicably, had his desire.

It was back!

Cesare's deep voice cut through the stretching silence. 'Leave us, Tim.'

Tim, who was walking across the room to Sam, stopped in his tracks at the curt request. Cesare could feel the other man's astonished stare, but ignored it.

'Leave you?' Tim echoed as if he couldn't

quite believe what he was hearing. His glance slid to Sam. 'With her?'

'Yes.' One corner of Cesare's mouth lifted and he sketched a sardonic smile.

Sam's sense of insecurity deepened. She had mentally prepared herself to expect one thing, but this wasn't it! Not only had Cesare's appearance undergone a transformation, so had his manner.

The Cesare Brunelli in Scotland had been struggling with demons of self-doubt as he came to terms with what had happened to him. He had been angry and frustrated, his manner abrasive and belligerent.

This man, with his air of unstudied authority, looked as if he'd never experienced a moment of self-doubt in his life!

'I'll call if I feel in danger, Tim.'

And what will I do if I feel in danger? Sam thought as she drew a deep breath. She already felt in danger—of losing her mind if nothing else.

This is what I wanted, she reminded herself. But suddenly being alone with Cesare Brunelli no longer seemed so desirable.

'Hold on, Tim,' Cesare ordered, and Tim paused. 'What does she look like?'

'Pardon?'

'Is she a blue-eyed blonde, a brown-eyed brunette…?'

Cesare already knew that her face was level with his heart, he knew that her figure was correspondingly petite and the skin that covered those delicious slight curves was smooth and silky. It was a shock for him to recognise how often during the intervening weeks he had thought of the face he had traced with his fingers, the face with the small, determined chin, tip-tilted nose and wide, lush mouth. His musing had been frustrated by the inability to put a colour to her eyes or to know the shade of the long silky tresses he had speared his fingers into and smoothed from her brow.

'She has deep blue eyes—very blue—and auburn hair,' Tim said, without looking to check the details. He then looked embarrassed and threw Sam a self-conscious and apologetic look. 'Sorry.'

Sam shook her head. 'It isn't *you* who has no manners.' Neither did he have an aura of raw sexuality that made it impossible for a person to relax in his company.

The pointed comment drew a hastily cut-off chuckle from Tim, who then quickly vanished.

The door closed with a click and she took a deep breath. 'I'm…'

Cesare tilted his head to one side. Red hair explained the temper and meshed perfectly with his mental image. 'I know who you are, *cara*. You seem to have made quite an impression on Timothy,' he stated, not looking entirely pleased by this observation. 'So a blue-eyed redhead…?'

'I hardly think the colour of my eyes is relevant.'

'Possibly, but as we are on such *intimate* terms… Now, I don't think we were ever formally introduced…Sam…?'

To his mind a boy's name was entirely inappropriate for the most feminine woman he had ever encountered.

'How did you know that it was me?' She shook her head and directed her wary gaze at his face. 'You couldn't, you can't…' Unless…?

She took a stumbling step backwards as he began to cross the room towards her, moving with confidence as he negotiated his route past several obstacles including a chair that stood in his way.

If she hadn't known already it would never have crossed her mind that he was blind.

Maybe he wasn't any longer?

His next mocking words revealed he had read her thoughts.

'I may be blind, *cara*, but I'm not stupid.'

But I am, she thought as she stared at his mouth and thought about it on her skin… She shivered and wrapped her arms around herself protectively. She was glad that he could not see the giveaway action.

'Then how?'

'Your voice is very distinctive.' Low and smoky with a sexy little rasp. The muscles along his taut jaw tightened as his resentment stirred. Like an annoying tune, he hadn't been able to get that husky sound out of his head.

Or her.

Sam's fingers clenched and she said quickly, 'A lot of people have a Scottish accent.'

But only one had that voice.

Cesare had not doubted for one second that this was the woman who had spent that night in Scotland with him. 'And your perfume…'

He swallowed hard, causing a visible wave of contraction beneath the brown skin of his throat. His nostrils flared as his body responded to the warm floral female scent in his nostrils.

'I don't use perfume,' she protested hoarsely.

He had stopped close enough so that all she had to do was reach out and she could touch him, and she felt an almost overwhelming compulsion to do just that.

This was crazy! She hadn't come here to revisit this insanity, Sam thought as she gulped and tried to tear her eyes from his beautiful face. She failed—the man was totally compelling.

'And now the mystery woman has a name…' The indentation between his eyebrows deepened. *'Sam…?'*

The way he wrapped his tongue around her name sent an illicit shiver down her spine.

'Samantha, but everyone calls me Sam.'

'I prefer Samantha.'

Sam was wondering how to respond to that

when without warning he stretched out his hand. She closed her eyes and swayed as the sensitive tips of his long brown fingers trailed slowly down the curve of her cheek.

'So you are real. I was beginning to wonder, but for the scratches on my back I might have decided you were a figment of my imagination.'

The hot, mortified colour flew to Sam's cheeks as she lowered her gaze, unable to maintain eye contact even though he couldn't see her.

'Look, I expect you're wondering why I'm here.' She'd started to wonder much the same thing herself… This was something that could have been done at a distance—clinically.

But then you wouldn't have seen him, pointed out the sly voice in her head, *and isn't that what you really wanted…?*

Cesare shook his head. 'No, I assume you want something. I'd like to flatter myself and think it is my body, but…'

A choking sound escaped Sam's throat. 'You're really not that fantastic,' she told him as the erotic images playing in her head stood witness to her whopper of a lie.

'That's not what you said at the time… "Perfect, utterly perfect" were words mentioned several times, I think, and you also appeared to have a very high opinion of my abilities in bed.'

'If you were any sort of a gentleman you wouldn't have brought that up.'

'I'm not.'

She shook her head. 'Not what?'

Her stomach muscles clenched as the corners of his lips lifted in a slow predatory smile. 'A gentleman, *cara*, not in any sense of the word, but then it wasn't my beautiful manners that made you jump into bed with me, was it?'

'I can't believe I ever felt sorry for you!' she gasped, glaring at him.

His head went back as though she had struck him. With nostrils flared and a thin white line etched around the sculpted outline of his lips, he retorted in a voice edged with ice, 'So you slept with me because you felt sorry for me?'

Sam's brow puckered into a frown as she returned to a mystery she had still not fully resolved to her own satisfaction. 'I really don't know why I did it—I'm always so sensible.' She gave a perplexed shake of her head and sighed. 'I knew what I was doing, I knew it was crazy, but it was as if…'

As he listened to her faltering response the hostility drained from Cesare's expression. 'You just had to in the same way you had to take your next breath.'

Sam looked up, amazed to hear her own feelings so simply but accurately expressed. 'Exactly like that!' Then, realising what she had just admitted and to whom she had admitted it, she blushed to the roots of her hair and added defensively, 'I don't feel sorry for you any more.'

The wolflike smile that revealed his even white teeth made Sam wonder if she had been too subtle in her effort to make the point that the madness had passed and she no longer felt unable to control herself.

'But we are forgetting the formalities, Samantha.' He said her name as though testing the taste of it on his tongue before inclining his dark head and announcing formally, 'I am Cesare. But of course you already know this…you are here. The only question remaining is still why?'

The why was something she was still working her way around to. 'I didn't know your name when I…when we…'

'Went to bed because you were consumed by pity—I must say you hid it well.'

The sardonic insertion brought a flush to her cheeks. 'Oh, I didn't feel it then, not until I saw your picture in an article.' She had not believed for a moment that the man described as the financial genius of his generation was the same man she had spent the night with. Then she had read the brief paragraph that mentioned an accident that had robbed him of his sight and the subsequent calling-off of his marriage to a well-known actress.

'And now you have discovered a new depth of feeling for me?'

Sam, baffled by the ironic suggestion, shook her head. 'I…'

'Now you deeply regret, in hindsight, leaving while I was sleeping?'

The guilty colour climbed to Sam's cheeks. 'That was… I…' How could she explain the fact that she had been too embarrassed to hang around, that she'd never woken up beside a man before and she had panicked?

'No need for explanations—I understand this change of heart totally.'

'I doubt that,' she muttered drily.

'Oh, yes, I know from experience how people's attitudes change when they discover how much money I have.'

It took the space of several seconds for Sam's brain to translate the sarcasm. Teeth clenched, she levelled an angry, glittering violet-blue-eyed glare at his lean, sardonic face.

A man who had such a jaundiced view of human nature was not likely to greet the news he had fathered a child with an open mind.

'For the record, I don't care about your money.'

Cesare was conscious of a feeling of irrational disappointment as he dragged a hand through his dark hair—she was the same as everyone else after all.

What was her angle?

Cesare had never been a man who indulged in one-night stands and he considered men who slipped away like thieves in the night were displaying at the very least bad manners. He saw no reason not to apply the same rules to women.

And while her walking out on him had initially made him as mad as hell, once the anger had worn off he had realised she had just given and not asked for anything in return, which in his world made her pretty unique. Alas it now seemed that she was not so special.

'Of course you don't.'

His cynical drawl made her want to hit him. 'And if I was as cynical as you…' She drew a deep breath and bit back the retort, forcing herself to continue with more moderation as she added honestly, 'I really had no idea who you were when I…we…at the time, and quite honestly I wish I still didn't. But I was researching for an article and your photo…'

'Researching…?'

Sam misread the edge in his voice as skepticism and she raised her chin in defence.

'Actually, I work for the *Chronicle*,' she said, trying to sound casual and failing—she still got a buzz from people looking impressed when she told them her job.

Cesare did not look impressed. In fact he couldn't have looked *less* impressed. 'You're a journalist?'

'Yes…' Hearing the defensive note in her voice, she bit her lip and added, 'I happen to be very good at what I do.'

'I do not doubt it.'

His sneer left her in no doubt that this comment was not intended as a compliment.

'I take it you have a problem with journalists.'

Cesare bared his teeth in a snarling smile, giving himself a moment to contain the fury he could feel hammering inside his skull before he responded in a voice that was wiped clean of all emotion save contempt.

'I suppose it is a job that would suit someone with no moral scruples.' The person who had interviewed the family of the child he had pulled from the burning car had certainly had nothing that approached a moral. They had added to the anguish by asking the parents while their child lay critically ill if they felt responsible for Cesare's own loss of sight.

The careless observation drew a gasp of startled anger from Sam's lips.

'I try not to generalise and I admit that most journalists I know would stop short of lying their way into someone's bed to get a juicy story,' Cesare said, shaking his head. 'I should have, but you know I didn't see this one coming… I should have known there is no such thing as a free lunch.'

An open-handed slap landed with a resounding crack on the side of his face, the force of the blow sending his head sideways.

Shame and shock rolled over Sam as she pressed both hands to her heaving chest. She had just seen red when he made that snide remark. It might not have been deep and meaningful to him, but he didn't have to trivialise and make the night sound so cheap and nasty.

She was shaking. She had never struck anyone in anger in her life…it wasn't in her nature.

Just as it wasn't in her nature to have a one-night stand.

It was this man! Tears of frustration swam in her eyes as he added insult to injury by laughing.

'You think this is funny?'

One hand laid against the red mark on his lean

cheek, he lifted his broad shoulders in an expressive shrug. 'At last,' he drawled, 'I've found a woman who doesn't make any concessions to my disability. If only you weren't also a callous, manipulative little bitch you might well be the perfect PA…or even,' he added, his voice dropping an octave to become so sexy and suggestive that a flash of heat was sent across the surface of Sam's skin, 'the perfect mistress.'

'If that's the post you're interviewing for I can see why you're struggling to fill it!' she snarled, thinking how a job like that would have them queuing around the block! 'No wonder your fiancée left you!'

She watched as he tilted his head slowly to one side. There was no suggestion in his expression that the jibe had hurt him, but she felt a surge of guilt anyway.

'It was in the article I read,' she admitted gruffly. And she, like, she suspected, most of the people reading it, had not for one second believed that the separation between the glamorous couple had preceded the accident that had left the billionaire blind.

'And I was downstairs when Candice...so are things all right between you now?'

Her fishing trip went unrewarded. 'Is this professional interest?'

There was that sardonic inflection in his voice again. 'Your love life doesn't interest me professionally or otherwise.' Though she seemed to be doing a pretty good impression of someone who did care. 'I'm sorry,' she added, feeling the focus of her anger shifting to the woman who had left the man she loved when he needed her.

What kind of woman did that?

A beautiful one, she thought as an image of the blonde actress in the sexy red dress formed in her head. Sam had put the immediate strong wave of antipathy she had felt towards the article's photo of the actress smiling up at Cesare down to the strong resemblance the woman had to the one Will had dumped her for. Now Sam had seen Candice in the flesh she knew that she had been doing the actress an injustice. She was far more beautiful in reality, oddly enough, also more real was the antipathy that Sam felt towards her.

The pity in Sam's apology caused Cesare's brows to twitch into a straight line.

'You are sorry for what?' he enquired warily.

'Well, that she left you, of course!' Sam retorted, her voice cracking with dislike and aggravation as she immediately contradicted herself by adding, 'Though I don't blame her, because you may be blind but you're still a total bastard. You know, I *really* wish that I had slept with you for a story…because if I had I would be feeling a lot less stupid now!' she declared shrilly.

'Then if not for a story, why did you sleep with me?'

Sam ignored the question. She'd had practice— she'd been doing just that to the ones in her own mind for the last twelve weeks. 'You think I'd write about what happened? You think I want to advertise the fact I slept with you! You think I want my family and friends to know?' She shook her head and told him grimly, 'Nothing could be farther from the truth. I'm *ashamed* of what I did!'

Having listened to her emotional diatribe with an expression approaching boredom, he leapt on her last comment.

'You think sex is something to be ashamed of?'

The suggestion brought an angry flush to her cheeks.

'Only sex with you! I've had relationships—I was engaged.' *He really does not need to know this,* she told herself.

'Engaged?' For some unfathomable reason Cesare experienced a flash of searing anger at the image that went with this statement.

'Yes, engaged! For your information I have a perfectly healthy attitude to sex! I'm not some sort of repressed...' She stopped, just managing to cut her retort short of total suicidal disclosure—it turned out she needn't have bothered.

CHAPTER THREE

'VIRGIN?' As Cesare spoke the memory of Sam's hoarse cry of wonder echoed in his head, but as the memory dredged up feelings he did not want to examine he pushed it away.

Now, the suggestion drew a strangled cry of dismay from her throat.

He arched a dark brow. 'You thought I wouldn't notice?'

'Hoped.' Sam bit her lip as the admission escaped uncensored.

'So you could pretend it didn't happen? Do you intend to be a professional virgin?' he goaded. 'The next time you decide to offer me psychological advice, remember that you are the well-balanced woman who preferred anonymous sex with a stranger than to sleep with her fiancé.'

'I don't prefer anonymous sex!' She was outraged at the suggestion.

'Then you did know who I was.'

A hissing sound of exasperation escaped her clamped lips. 'I keep telling you I had no idea who you were.'

'The dictionary definition of anonymous sex is carnal relations with someone you don't know.'

'You don't read the same dictionaries I do. Look, I really don't know why you're making such a big thing of this… Honestly, to hear you talk anyone would think I drugged you into submission. It just happened, and I'm not going to beat myself up over it.' That sounded really grown up—in a perfect world she really would be this well balanced and pragmatic. 'And for the record I'd have been quite happy to have sex, it was Will who…' She stopped, an expression of mortified horror spreading across her face as she realised what she had said.

'Your fiancé wouldn't sleep with you?' Cesare thought of her soft body beneath him, of her pulling him down towards her.

There was no question in his mind that any

man who could have had that and rejected it was a fool—a certifiable loser.

'He fell in love with someone else and my personal life is none of your business,' she hissed, wishing she had realised this *before* she had blabbed all the embarrassing details.

'Tell me what else am I to think? You turned up out of nowhere, pretending to be a *cleaner*... You tried to get inside my head...'

'Believe me, your head is the very last place I'd want to be.'

'You say you didn't want to be in my bed but that's where you ended up. Where you planned to end up?'

The totally unjustified suggestion drew a cry of protest from Sam. 'I did no such thing! I didn't plan anything, it...it was an accident. It was sympathy sex,' she was driven to claim.

The words were barely out of her mouth when she was racked by shame and guilt. It had been a mean and petty thing to say, not to mention a lie, but there were times, she told herself, when only a lie worked, and she felt desperate.

Frustratingly her pitiless assertion did not even

dent his self-assurance, let alone do irreparable damage to his self-esteem, which looked to be fully intact. He even laughed before he drawled, 'Sure it was, *cara*.'

She watched his expressive mouth curl upwards, then swallowed as she closed her eyes and remembered feeling the hot, carnal caresses of his mouth on her. A shiver passed through her body and she thought how it was better by far not to go there.

'A second ago I was capable of sleeping with you for a story, but suddenly I slept with you because you're utterly irresistible. Maybe I was just curious?' He greeted the suggestion with an arched brow. 'I'd never slept with a blind man before.'

'You'd never slept with any man before.'

'Then I hope it makes you feel special!' she yelled. 'You know, I don't know why you're so mad with me. Unless it's because you resent that I saw through the macho tough-guy façade. Don't worry, I know what happened wasn't personal.'

'Not personal?'

'You needed someone and I was there.'

Cesare frowned and pushed away the intrusive memory of the feelings that had twisted in his chest when he'd held her in his arms in the breathless aftermath of their lovemaking. The knowledge that he had been her first lover had shocked him, but it had also deeply aroused him, more than he had imagined possible.

'It is true there have always been some things, *cara*, that I prefer not to do alone—'

The deliberate crudity made her blush.

'It's a foible of mine and if we're talking needs I'd say that you needed me at least as much as I needed you. Will you put that in your story? Is this is a courtesy visit to inform me of the imminent article? I'm interested—what tack did you take…?'

'Go to hell!' she choked.

'Which is where I was when you dragged me back from the edge by sharing your delicious little body with me. An interesting angle for you—how I saved the billionaire on the brink by generously sharing my luscious little body. But I have to tell you it was only sex—you were not my salvation.' It was something he had told himself on more than one occasion.

'Believe me, I wouldn't want to be!' she was able to rebut with total sincerity.

'What are you, then?'

The words slipped out before she could stop them. 'Pregnant. I'm twelve weeks pregnant.'

In the act of straightening his already perfectly symmetrical silk tie, Cesare froze. For several seconds he did nothing at all including, or so it seemed to Sam, breathe.

'Pregnant?'

'It was quite a shock.'

Cesare's heartbeat and the world around seemed to have slowed. 'You're sure?'

The question sent a surge of anger through her. 'You think this is something I would say if I wasn't absolutely sure? You think I just came here on the off chance?' She stopped and blinked back the sudden rush of tears that filled her eyes. Of course I'm sure!' she added thickly.

'You're crying!' Cesare accused.

'No, I'm not,' she denied, shaking her head as he scrubbed a hand across her pink nose.

Through her damp lashes she watched as he speared his fingers into his hair and rested the heels of his hands against his closed eyes.

'I don't know about you, but I don't see any need for a post-mortem over why and how and—'

His head lifted. 'I think we both know how.'

His wry interruption brought a dull flush to Sam's pale cheeks. She bit her lip, lifted her chin and continued doggedly as though he had not spoken.

'The why still remains something of a mystery to me, but,' she added adopting a bright tone, 'these things happen…' She stopped and bit her lip again. Couldn't she say anything that wasn't a cliché or a platitude?

A muscle clenched in his lean cheek. 'Not to me.'

'Well, me neither, as it happens.'

'Do you think I don't know that?' He hadn't just impregnated a woman, he had impregnated a virgin! In some societies that could be a capital offence.

'Look, don't worry, I'm not expecting anything from you. I just thought you might like to know…so now you do I'll be off…' She shrugged the strap of her bag firmer onto her shoulder and turned.

'You'll be off…?' he choked.

'Yes.'

His shook his head. 'This is surreal…'

Sam knew what he was talking about. 'Hard to take on board all at once, I know, but I'll just leave you my number in case you want to contact me.' He would probably throw it in the waste-paper bin when she left, but she had done the right thing in telling him.

'Who *are* you?'

'You know who I am, I'm Sam Muir.'

He shook his head impatiently. 'I mean *who*…why were you cleaning at that place that night? A cold, drafty castle in the middle of nowhere.' Cesare had only noticed the cold after she had gone. 'The woman I spoke to the next day…'

'Clare—my sister-in-law. I asked her not to—' She could hear the strident ring of a phone somewhere in the distance and it seemed strange to Sam that normal things were happening in other parts of the building while she was experiencing the most abnormal moment of her life. She would never complain about mundane or routine again.

'Be cooperative about your whereabouts?' Cesare finished for her suggestively.

'Even if I hadn't asked her to be discreet, she wouldn't pass on the details of any employee to a stranger.'

'Discreet? The woman invented some crazy story about epidemics.'

'That's not a lie, it's the truth. Look, if you must know, I don't make a habit of having one-night stands with total strangers and I left because I was…embarrassed.' Sam recalled the burning shame she had felt when she had awoken with a man's face cushioned on her breasts.

Her heavy eyelids closed and her eyelashes fluttered against her flushed cheeks as things low and deep inside tightened and quivered. She was able to recollect in exact detail how the heat of his breath on her skin had felt and the sensual, abrasive roughness of his jaw against the ultra-sensitive flesh.

Even filled with total horror and self-loathing at the situation she had been unable to resist the temptation to sink her fingers into the lush thickness of his hair and smooth the strands back from his brow before she had carefully extricated herself.

'So you're related to the people who run the Armuirn Estate?' Cesare asked.

Sam nodded, then remembered he couldn't see her. 'Yes, by marriage. Clare and my brother run the estate. He was ill that night with the flu. So there was a flu epidemic. I stepped in as a cleaner to help them out.'

'The man you spoke of when we were together that evening…Ian, is it? He is your brother?' Cesare could remember feeling an irrational spurt of hostility to the man she had casually referred to.

Sam, who couldn't recall having mentioned Ian at all, said, 'Yes. He and Clare can't afford to live in the castle. They have twin boys, but you really don't want to know any of this, do you?'

If the man didn't want to know about his own child he was hardly going to be much interested in the offspring of total strangers.

His voice, deep and impatient, cut across her. 'Look, maybe you should sit back down?'

'I'm fine as I am.'

'Maybe I'll sit down, then.'

She watched as he folded his long, lean length into a chair and sat there with his chin rested on steepled fingers.

The silence stretched.

Finally he broke it. 'This isn't a joke—you're actually pregnant?'

Sam caught herself in the act of nodding again and bit her lip. 'Yes.'

She waited tensely.

He looked pale, but, considering the bombshell she had just dropped, he appeared to be taking it pretty well, if you discounted that muscle in his lean cheek that was spasmodically throbbing.

'Did you plan this?'

Sam stiffened. 'I beg your pardon?'

The ice crystals in her normally expressive voice gave him a pretty clear idea of what she was feeling. The frustration of not being able to see her face was like a dull ache in his chest. There had been many bitter moments since he'd become blind when he had grieved for the loss of his sight, but never had he felt it as acutely as he did at this moment.

'You think I planned this?'

'It is a possibility.' Even as he spoke he recognised his own lack of conviction.

'Only if you have a warped mind, but don't worry, I don't want anything from you. It just seemed…polite to let you know.'

'Polite?'

'If I'd known you were some sort of weird conspiracy-theorist nut I wouldn't have bothered. You obviously think that all women are out to get impregnated by you… Well, let me tell you, from where I'm standing you don't look like such a bargain,' she snorted contemptuously. 'Unless you like cynical, mean-minded and plain nasty. For the record, if I could have chosen a father for my baby it really wouldn't be you! You wouldn't even make the shortlist. So go ahead, think this was all part of some cunning plan, and feel happy because if it was it definitely backfired!'

He heard the lock on the door click and

realised she was walking out on him again. Rage rose up in him, closely followed by something he refused to recognise as panic.

'Marry me.'

The flat statement—it could hardly be called a request—delivered in that terse, peremptory tone effectively ruined her sweeping exit and almost made Sam fall off her high heels.

She slowly turned her head. 'You'll laugh, but—' He didn't laugh, though, or even smile as she stared, unable to tear her eyes from his dark features. Not a muscle in his face moved and his beautiful eyes somehow remained focused on her own face.

Sam turned her head and told herself the feeling of something hard and heavy lodged behind her breastbone was pity. The sort she would feel for anyone who had suffered such a tragedy.

'For a moment there I thought you said…'

'Do not play games. You heard me, Samantha.'

Her headmistress had been the only other person to call her Samantha, but it had not made her nerve endings prickle or even lightly tingle.

She swallowed, her voice rising to an incredulous squeak as she asked on a note of hysterical query, 'You're proposing we get *married*?'

'Is that not what you wanted me to say?' Cesare, who had been almost as surprised as she appeared to be to hear himself make the proposal, could now see that it was the obvious solution—the *only* solution. 'Is that not why you came here?'

Sam's eyes went saucer-wide—he sounded so incredibly matter of fact about the subject.

'I never in a million years expected you to suggest this…or wanted you to,' she added, thinking of and instantly dismissing those few silly fantasies she had been guilty of weaving in the middle of the previous interminably long sleepless night. Fantasies were harmless—things only got dangerous when you started trying to act them out.

'Look, I don't know if you're actually serious—'

'It is not a subject I am likely to joke about.'

Despite the outraged note of offence in his interjection, Sam was not so sure. This man's personality and the motives that drove him were still pretty much an enigma to her—ironic considering that he knew her more intimately than any man. At her side her fists clenched as she struggled not to think about *how* intimately.

'But don't you think this is a slight overreaction?' He couldn't see her so he wouldn't know how badly she failed in her attempt at a smile—it was cold comfort when she was shaking hard from the inside out. As if things weren't already complicated enough, he had to throw a crazy idea like this into the mix…and make her think about how different this would be if what they had shared had not been just sex.

'To a situation as trivial as having my child, you mean?'

'*Our* child.' His sudden possessive attitude was something that made Sam uneasy and something she definitely didn't want to encourage.

He dismissed the correction with a fluid shrug. 'I have some old-fashioned idea about family life.'

'I'm sure your girlfriend might have some too. Look, I'm not treating this trivially, I'm just trying to make life easier on you. I'm not making any unreasonable demands.'

'You should be,' he said. Sam was still struggling to make sense of his condemnation when his
distinctive dark brows drew together in an irritated
frown of incomprehension. *'Girlfriend…?'*

Will he dismiss me *from his thoughts as
simply when I walk from the room?* Sam
wondered bleakly.

'Candice was leaving as I arrived.'

'Candice need not concern you.'

'She might have something to say about you
marrying someone else.' Probably very loudly,
too. To people like the actress, publicity was a
way of life. To Sam the idea of her personal life
becoming the currency of gossip columns filled
her with utter horror.

An expression of baffled irritation settled on
Cesare's features. He moved his right hand in a
dismissive arc. 'What has it to do with her?'

'Or me, I suppose?' she suggested, utterly
appalled by his display of callous unconcern for
his ex-lover…maybe not even ex…? The man
was clearly as ruthless in his personal life as he
was reputed to be in business.

'Do not be ridiculous!'

The suggestion drew a laugh of sheer incredulity from her throat. 'Me ridiculous?' she echoed, laying her palm flat against her heaving chest. 'I'm not the one saying we should get married. For God's sake, you didn't know my name until a few minutes ago!' She lifted a hand to her brow and shook her head. This entire situation was beyond surreal and the scary thing was that for a split second she had almost started to consider it.

'But I knew a lot of other things about you, Samantha.'

The sexual inference in his deep drawl sent a flash of heat over her skin. 'You don't know me at all,' she snapped back, her anger divided between him and herself. Why did she let him do this to her?

He ignored her statement and asked, 'Are you worried a blind man would not make a good father?'

The frustrating thought of the many things he would never be able to do with his child rose in Cesare's head to torment him. He realised he would never see his child's face and the acknowledgement was like a knife thrust to his heart.

'You being blind has got nothing to do with it,' Sam said. 'They say that women are instinctively drawn to alpha males to father their children.' Up until now Sam had been able to say she was the exception to the rule. 'And as you're about the most alpha male on the planet…'

'A man who requires guidance to cross the road cannot protect his child from danger.' It was a father's role to guard his offspring from the perils in the world, and the thought of this role reversal filled Cesare with a furious impotence.

Sam studied his self-critical expression and felt her tender heart twist as she recognised the fear and doubts that lay under the confident front he presented to the world.

'Being blind does not make you a bad father or role model.' Unlike, to her way of thinking, sleeping with blonde actresses with long legs. 'It has nothing to do with this situation at all, except,' she admitted, adhering reluctantly to honesty, 'that if you had been able to see none of this would have happened.'

'You mean I would not have been in Scotland that night.'

'I mean you would have been able to see me,' she blurted. Irritated by his blank frown, she spelt it out. 'I'm not your type.'

She saw the flicker at the back of his eyes and wished she had let him continue to carry the clearly unrealistic image he had of her, but as tempting as it was, she couldn't.

'I think you should let me be the judge of that. I have seen your face with my fingers.' Eyes half closed, his fingers inscribed a series of soft motions in the air.

Sam found the contemplative smile that curled one corner of his mouth deeply disturbing. 'You could do the same with your child.'

His hands fell and something she could not read flickered across his face. His deep voice fell softly and it carried a note she could not interpret. 'So I could.'

'I have freckles.'

The abrupt insertion drew a grin from him.

'Seriously,' she stressed.

'That of course alters things,' he said with a

wry smile. Then his expression grew solemn before he released a hissing sound of frustration between his teeth and wondered angrily, 'Has this fiancé who cheated and rejected you given you such a low opinion of yourself?'

The suggestion startled Sam. 'No! I was never in love with Will.' And she was sharing with him the realisation that had taken her months to recognise because…?

'Well, it is true. You are not my type.'

Sam was glad he could not see her flinch.

'But not because of any imagined physical template you appear to imagine I expect my sexual partners to conform to. You are not my type because you are incredibly high maintenance.'

The accusation robbed her briefly of the ability to speak. 'Me? High maintenance?'

'Yes, you. Also I do not have relationships with women who need me to tell them they are beautiful.'

'I do not—!'

He cut back in before she could complete her hot rebuttal of this outrageous claim. 'I do not have relationships with women who never lose an opportunity to point out my myriad flaws.'

'And yet you still want to marry me—only you don't really, do you.' She paused and he didn't speak. She'd have thought less of him if he had. She thought less of herself because she wanted him to. Struggling to rationalise the irrational desire to hear him lie, she lifted her chin.

'Look, I'm sure you'd be—will be—a great father, blind or not, but you'd be an awful husband and I don't want to be married to a man who doesn't love me.'

His cynical smile deepened as he heard her out. 'So love conquers all?'

'Maybe not, but despite my apparent lack of self-esteem I'm not settling for second best.'

Cesare, suffering from the shock of hearing himself called second best, heard the door open.

In his head the memories he had been holding back surfaced with merciless accuracy to taunt him. He remembered running his fingers over the surface of her belly and feeling the fine network of muscle beneath the soft skin quiver. Tracing the curved angle of her hip with his hands, drawing the tight little swollen buds of her delicious breasts into his mouth and hearing her beg him not to stop. Kissing the hollow at the base of her throat where the echo of her heartbeat had passed from her to him through his fingertips and lips.

It was ironic. She was the only woman he had slept with but never seen and he carried a more vivid memory of her body than anyone else's before.

It took seconds for the images and tactile sensations that went with them to flash through his mind, but it was long enough to make his body burn with the strength of his out-of-control arousal.

Teeth clenched, Cesare leapt up from his chair, a growl that registered too low for human ears vibrating in his chest as he stalked towards the door. He was actually in the act of tearing it open when he stopped himself. What the hell was he doing?

His breathing slowed. The damned little witch was running out on him again and he was following—straight down a stairwell probably in this sort of temper. He decided if she ran and he followed it was not a good message to send out.

Not if a man wanted to maintain the illusion at least of being in control.

Face set in a dark scowling mask of discontent, he turned and walked back to his chair.

CHAPTER FOUR

IT BEGAN to rain just as the taxi drew up on the kerb. It only took seconds for Sam to reach the waiting vehicle, but by the time she closed the door on the downpour her hair was drenched, despite the bag she had held over her head to shield her.

She looked out the window and her thoughts were drawn irresistibly back to her weekend break in Scotland—it had been raining like this that last day.

Sam had read no sinister portents into the gathering storm clouds, she had had no inkling that her life was about to change as she drew the Land Rover up on the gravelled forecourt of the Armuirn Castle.

She had simply been doing a favour for her harassed sister-in-law and about the only thing that had been on her mind was a nice hot bath. She had not anticipated that the cleaning of eight cottages would be so physically strenuous. Not that she had had any intention of letting on and confirming her brother's mocking opinion that city life had made her soft.

She had shaded her eyes and tilted her head as she'd looked at the castellated turret. The grey-stoned landmark could be seen for miles around. It had been her sister-in-law's childhood home, but these days Ian and Clare lived in one of the farms and rented out the big house along with several crofts to tourists.

Sam had lugged out a basket containing the cleaning materials, thinking how wielding a feather duster and changing bedlinen hadn't *quite* been the way she had viewed spending her holiday. But she could hardly have gone off hiking in the hills when a virulent flu bug had had her sister-in-law so short-staffed that she'd been trying to do ten jobs as well as look after two-year-old twins.

Though Sam had pronounced herself willing to do anything, she had actually been relieved when the *anything* had not involved looking after the twins. She loved her nephews dearly, but the responsibility of keeping that fearless pair amused and safe was not a responsibility she felt equipped to deal with.

Instead a guilty and grateful Clare had asked if she would clean and prepare the cottages on changeover day for the new intake of holiday-makers and, if she had time, take a grocery order up to the castle and change the linen there.

When Sam had asked if she should run a duster around the place Clare had said definitely not. It seemed the man who had rented the castle for the summer did not want housekeeping.

In fact he did not want anything except total privacy.

Sam had been curious. 'What's he like?'

'Don't ask me. I've never even seen him, neither has Ian. The booking was taken via the website.'

'Someone must have seen him,' Sam protested. This was after all an incredibly close-knit community where everyone knew everyone's business.

'Oh, Hamish got a glimpse. He was taking some climbers that way when a helicopter put down.'

'And?' Sam prompted.

'Our mystery man got out. Hamish said he was tall.'

'Not helpful.'

Clare nodded in agreement. 'Nobody has seen him up close since. He stays in the castle, he doesn't come into the village. He leaves a grocery list for us when we go in with fresh towels and such like, but we haven't seen him either.'

'Maybe he's a fugitive hiding from the authorities or a film star in the middle of a sex scandal escaping the tabloids?'

'More likely he's a stressed executive here for the fishing. But whoever he is give him a wide berth, Sam. The man has taken the castle for six months and he's paid upfront so if he wants to be invisible he can be.'

'So does the invisible man have a name?'

'I don't recall…it was foreign. Spanish or Italian, I think…?'

By the time Sam reached the castle it was turned six and her interest in the tall Mediterranean had waned. She was shattered. She had changed twenty beds and vacuumed acres of carpet not to mention cleaned windows and been stung by a wasp. All she wanted was to get back to the farm and put her feet up.

There was no sign of the antisocial guest and no response when she poked her head around the door and called out before she went into the kitchen.

Inside the kitchen was dark, the blinds drawn. She put the box of groceries on the floor and after a short fumble found the light switch.

'Oh, my God!' Sam's horrified gaze travelled around the room. It was a total disaster zone, with dirty plates and glasses everywhere plus open cartons and cans. There was not a clean surface in the room. A quick examination of the fridge where Clare had asked her to leave the perishable items revealed most of the contents were either out of date or unrecognisable and growing things.

Sam thought of the hot bath and sighed as she rolled up her sleeves. She was no tidiness freak, and minimalism was not her thing—she liked a bit of cosy clutter—but this was something else entirely.

If the man didn't want housekeeping, well, too bad, she thought. In the interests of hygiene alone she couldn't leave it as it was.

Half an hour later the place still wouldn't have made a health inspector smile, but it was a distinct improvement. She folded her arms across her chest and gave a small nod of satisfaction as she placed the last empty bottle in the sack for recycling and said out loud, 'Well, I just hope he appreciates this.'

'Who the hell are you and what are you doing here?'

A fractured gasp of shock left her lips as hands closed over her shoulders and spun her around.

Finding herself face to face with the middle button of a blue chambray shirt, she tilted her face to see the person whose fingers were grinding into the sensitive flesh that covered her collarbones and who was obviously not grateful at all. She found herself staring wide-eyed into the face of the most beautiful man she had ever seen or imagined.

The sensory overload of looking at this much sheer perfection made her head spin. She knew she was staring like an idiot, but she couldn't have stopped if her life had depended on it.

He was tall, several inches above six feet, and

muscular but not in a bulky way. Lean and hard. He had Mediterranean colouring, and his hair was black. It curled low on his neck and fell across his high forehead. The bones of his face were strongly carved, with razor-sharp cheek-bones, a masterful aquiline nose, and the piratical shadow on his firm jaw failing to disguise the fact it was uncompromisingly male.

In fact the only things that *weren't* uncom-promisingly male about him were the extrava-gant length of his lashes and the full curve of his lower lip that was then compensated by the firmness of the upper, the effect so overtly sensual it made her stomach muscles quiver.

In a bid to stop looking, Sam found herself gazing directly into his eyes instead. She fought to draw a shaky breath. They were so dark they were almost black. Looking into them made her feel as though she were falling.

She quickly reminded herself of the mess in the kitchen. 'You should be grateful,' she choked, dragging her violet-blue eyes away from his face. Breathing fast and shallow to carry some much needed oxygen to her brain, she allowed her glance to dwell significantly on the hands curved over her upper arms, before tilting her head and risking a second peek at his face.

He didn't take the hint and it wasn't gratitude that was etched on the sculpted angles and planes of his sternly beautiful face, but anger. She could almost see the ripples in the air as it oozed from him.

Suspicion and hostility were being aimed at her, and the air between them almost visibly crackled with it.

'Would you mind letting me go?' Sam asked as she lifted her chin and thought how she couldn't let him see that he was scaring her. That was what he'd want.

A frown flickered across his features and a second later the grip on her shoulders loosened, though still didn't drop away.

A sigh of premature relief snagged in her throat as her glance drifted to his mouth and she felt things shift low in her stomach.

'Who are you?' he questioned.

Sam swallowed. She knew who she wasn't.

She wasn't a woman who became wide-eyed and inarticulate because she saw a beautiful man.

She was *definitely* not a woman who was attracted to danger, and if any man had ever spelt danger she was looking at him. Looking at him and feeling a lot of things she'd have been happier not to. Never in her life had any man elicited such a strong reaction from her.

He frightened and repelled her, but at the same time the flip side to this was a shameful excitement that was seductive as it coursed through her veins like wine. Sam felt intoxicated. She had never in her twenty-four years experienced any feeling so primal and raw.

'Speak up or I will…'

The threat in his deep voice broke her free of the thrall that had held her motionless. The isolation of the castle and the vulnerability of her situation hit her… What *would* he do…?

'Let me go!' Fear made her voice shrill as she began to struggle frantically against his restraining hands.

'Dio mio!' he gritted as she hit out wildly, one of her flailing fists making contact with his jaw. 'Will you be still, woman?'

Sam was still, but only because the energy had

drained abruptly from her body, leaving her shaking and weak-kneed.

'You're Italian,' she stated. His lightly accented voice was deep and vibrant.

'You're trespassing.'

'No, I'm only the cleaner, I just came to change the sheets.'

'The cleaner…?' He didn't sound convinced, but she was relieved to see that, though he still regarded her with suspicion, some of the aggressive hostility had seeped from his manner.

He straightened up to his full and intimidating height and Sam exhaled a shaky breath as his hands fell from her shoulders. Her step backwards brought the back of her legs in contact with the big rustic table in the middle of the room. She leaned into it and pushed her hands in a smoothing motion over her hair. They were still shaking, as was her voice as she retorted sarcastically, 'No, I'm an international jewel thief and my calling card is washing the dirty dishes…'

She was glad several feet now separated them. Up close and distractingly personal he really was too overwhelming. She no longer imagined she was in any physical danger from this man, but her mental safety was another matter. Whatever it was he projected she was susceptible to it. Every time she looked at him her mind went to mush, and the stuff happening to the rest of her body did not bear close examination.

She was deeply ashamed of her initial reaction to this brooding, bad-tempered Italian with his sinfully sexy mouth and chiselled cheekbones. She lowered her eyes from his face, conscious that she was close to drooling. *For God's sake, woman, show a bit of pride,* she chided herself angrily.

'Of course I'm the cleaner.' She moved her hand in a sweeping motion from her tousled head down to her sensible shoes. 'What do I look like?'

He could say she resembled a total wreck and he wouldn't be wrong, she reflected, thinking how silly and shallow it was to care what he thought of her appearance. Especially as she would not have secured a second glance from him under any other circumstances, even if she had been wearing her most alluring outfit.

But he did not take her invitation to look at her.

Instead his unblinking heavy-lidded regard stayed trained on her face as he observed, 'You do not smell like a cleaner.'

'What do cleaners smell like?'

A dark brow arched sardonically. 'You, presumably. I have never held one as close as a lover before.'

The comment made the blush under her skin deepen. 'You've never lived,' she replied, trying not to think about lovers and this man in the same sentence.

'A tempting thought,' he said, not looking tempted.

Which was rude.

'That wasn't an invitation.' As if she would hand out invitations to a man who looked like a dark fallen angel.

He angled a brow and looked even more as though he knew far too much about kissing.

'So that is not part of the service…?'

'I don't charge for kisses, just for mopping, and I only kiss people I like.'

His attention drifted to the window as he appeared to lose interest in the conversation.

Without looking at her, he dragged a hand through his dark hair. Sam was used to men not noticing her in a sexual way, but most didn't act as though she were invisible.

The silence lengthened. When he did speak she jumped. 'You raise a man's expectations and then you dash them down. So, Mrs Cleaner, you can take your mop and go home. The estate were informed prior to my arrival that I do not require housekeeping services.'

Sam was tempted to pass the buck and say she was just the hired help, but Clare had more than enough to cope with without complaints from rich guests. Instead she said, 'They told me the same thing, but you were both wrong.'

A look of total astonishment passed across his lean features. 'I was wrong?'

A smile fluttered on her lips, then faded as her glance strayed and the fluttering moved to low in her belly.

'You were,' she croaked, her eyes still glued to his mouth. 'You *definitely* need me.' Even before he arched an expressive brow the mortified colour had rushed to her cheeks.

'You sound very confident of your ability to satisfy my needs…'

'There is no call to be crude and sarcastic,' she choked. 'And actually I would prefer not to think about your needs!' But of course she was. 'What I meant was you definitely need house-keeping services unless you are planning to eat with your fingers or you're keen to contract food poisoning. I thought you'd have been grateful.' Her glance travelled around the room. 'The place looks a lot better than it did.'

'And I am meant to thank you? I knew where everything was.'

'Shall I throw a few empty bottles around the place to make you feel at home?'

'I could put my hand on anything as and when I needed it.' He swept his hand in an expressive circular motion and sent the row of freshly washed glasses she had lined up on the dresser flying with a crash. The unexpected noise of breaking glass was so loud that Sam cried out.

Then her mouth fell open as she realised the action had been totally deliberate. Sam stared at him in disbelief. 'I suppose you expect me to clear that up for you?' If so he could think again.

Teeth clenched, he glared at her, his face a mask of seething dislike. 'I do not require your assistance. I am more than capable of...' To emphasise his capability he brought the flat of his hand down on the dresser top.

'Oh, yeah, it really looks like it...' Her voice faded as he lifted his hand. Her stomach flipped as she saw the blood dripping from the jagged cut on his palm. 'Oh, my God!' she cried in horror. 'You stupid man, what have you done?'

His jaw clenched. 'Nothing.'

'You idiot—what did you think you were doing? You hit it directly on the glass...anyone would think you were blind.'

'I am.'

'Very funny,' she began, tilting her head up towards his and finding him staring at the wall above her head. The exasperation on her face was replaced by the horror of realization. It wasn't a sick joke; he was telling the truth.

'You can't see—you're blind!' Shame and shock in equal parts washed over her like icy water. Her lips quivered and inside her chest something tightened as she lifted a hand to her face and found it wet with inexplicable tears.

'I'm so sorry, I didn't realise.' Still not quite able to believe those beautiful eyes could not see her, she passed a hand in front of his face. He didn't blink, but reached out with dizzying speed and caught her wrist in his uninjured hand.

'Stop that. I've had enough empathy to last me a lifetime!' he snarled. 'I do not require your sympathy or your pity!'

Sam looked at the blood dripping onto the floor and clenched her teeth. 'I get it.'

His lip curled contemptuously. 'You get what?'

'I get that you're mad with me because I saw you being vulnerable. Don't worry, I don't feel extra special. You're obviously mad with the world. The fact is you're blind—'

She stopped as she saw shock move at the back of his eyes. 'You think I need some Mrs Mop to remind me of this fact?'

Sam gritted her teeth and carried on as though the bitter interruption had not occurred. 'So you can carry on ignoring it if you wish, but like the dirty dishes it's not going to go away. So if I might make a suggestion, why don't you stop acting like a gutless wonder and get on with it? Sure it isn't fair, but—shock horror—life isn't!'

She saw the disbelief chase across his face and felt a surge of recklessness.

'This is none of my business—'

'No, it isn't.'

Again she acted as though he had not spoken. 'Which is probably a good thing, because I don't really care what you say to me. Unlike the friends and family out there, the people who love you and who are no doubt right now worried sick about you…'

There would be a wife or a lover among them. A man who looked like him, a man who projected a force field of raw sexuality, would not live the life of a monk.

She dragged her eyes from the widening scarlet stain on his sleeve and struggled to maintain the role of impartial stranger as she tilted her face up to his thinking how beautiful the woman in his life must be.

The stupid man probably thought he was being

noble and strong by going it alone up here in the castle. His problem was he was too stubborn and proud to admit he needed help.

'Meanwhile,' she continued, waving her finger even though he was oblivious. 'You lick your wounds here like some…some injured animal.' He'd be a wolf, she thought, studying his lean, handsome face and feeling the inevitable flip of her sensitive stomach. 'My God, you're selfish!' she finished in disgust.

There was a look of stark incredulity stamped on his hard patrician features as he tilted his head to one side, a nerve clenched in his lean cheek as those stunning dark eyes stared straight at her.

It seemed impossible to Sam that he wasn't seeing her.

'Selfish!'

There was a flat, eerie calm in the echo that sent a shiver down her spine and made her think of her recent analogy. Wounded animals of any variety were dangerous, especially wolves.

Even when his temper wasn't frayed to the point of snapping, there was something edgy, unpredictable and almost combustible about this stranger.

If she had any sense she would be heading for the door, not standing here winding him up.

Just why was she making this her business? The fluttering of excitement low in her belly and the light-headed recklessness born of the excess adrenaline circulating in her bloodstream might be a clue… Sam frowned, not liking the conclusions thrown up by her rapid self-analysis, not liking the feelings this man stirred inside her.

Like and this man did not sit comfortably in the same thought. *Like* was tepid and he was a person who inspired the more extreme ends of the emotional spectrum!

Sam stuck out her chin even though the defiant gesture was wasted on him. 'It's nothing to me why you've come here, but it doesn't take a genius to see it wasn't for the climbing or fishing, and you don't look like someone looking for spiritual peace.' If he was he'd taken the wrong turn somewhere, she thought, studying the uncompromising set of his jaw and the clenching nerve throbbing in his hollow cheek.

'You speak with passion for someone who is so disinterested. You know, in my experience people who feel the need to sort out other people's lives frequently have no life of their own.'

'They do say that attack is the best form of defence. And actually I have a perfectly satisfactory life, thank you…not everyone needs a man to feel fulfilled.'

She stopped, annoyance flickering across her face as she realised she had already said too much.

'My life is not the subject here.' She injected ice into her reminder.

'But nonetheless fascinating.'

The sarcastic drawl made her lips tighten. She fought to keep the antipathy—which was growing by the second—from her voice as she retorted bluntly, 'If you carry on bleeding that way you won't have a life either.'

She frowned, finding it pretty hard to be objective as she looked at the widening scarlet pool on the floor. 'Ian keeps a first-aid kit in the Land Rover. I'll go and get it.'

'I do not need a ministering angel.'

Sam fixed him with a very un-angelic glare

and promised, 'Take my word for it, you do not bring out the angel in me.'

'Who is Ian?'

Her hand on the doorknob, Sam, surprised by the question, looked back over her shoulder. 'He's the man you rented this place from.'

His darkly delineated brows set at an angle lifted towards his hairline. 'You are on first-name terms with your boss?'

'Oh, we're a really egalitarian lot up here.' The hauteur in his manner suggested he would not invite such familiarities with his subordinates. Despite his present dishevelled appearance, he acted like a man who was used to barking out orders and having people jump. 'And you'd get on with Ian—he thinks I have no life either.' Her blue eyes narrowed as she considered the well-meaning interference of her sibling.

His matchmaking tactics were never very subtle, but what Ian and other concerned parties—she didn't include this stranger among their number—didn't seem to appreciate was that she hadn't thrown herself into work because her boyfriend had run off with another woman.

She threw herself into work because she enjoyed it.

She really was over Will. She wasn't even mad with him any more. She was mad with herself because she had always known deep down that this gorgeous guy hadn't really been in love with her. It hadn't been respect that had stopped him jumping into bed with her before they were married, but a total lack of interest in her sexually.

And when she'd seen what sort of woman Will was interested in sexually she could she why. Gisela, the divinely fair Nordic beauty he had met and married all in the space of two weeks, was almost six feet tall and had a body that any man would lust after.

Still looking over her shoulder, Sam now watched the Italian search and find a tea towel that he proceeded to apply firmly to his wound.

'It's nothing to me if you want to hide away like some sort of bearded recluse.' Sam was rather pleased at her wooden delivery—things had been getting far too heated and personal. Of course, if he had been able to see her flushed face it would have ruined the illusion of objective boredom totally.

But he couldn't.

Again things hurt inside as she felt an unwelcome wave of empathic pain for his loss. She had already worked out that sympathy would only make him more pigheadedly uncooperative so she kept her tone flat as she admitted, 'But I'm going to clean and dress that wound whether you like it or not.'

'Bearded…?'

She almost wanted to smile as he lifted a hand to his face and looked surprised as his fingers slid across the stubble on his hard jawline. It was ironic really—there were numerous men out there who carefully nurtured their designer stubble in an effort to achieve exactly the look of dark, dangerous dissipation this man had without trying.

'Call me selfish, but it would be bad for business if you went home feet first, and the estate is just about the only employer around here.'

'So you wish to tend my wounds because it would affect the local economy, not because you are a ministering angel.'

His amused sneer made her see red. 'If bloody-minded aggression and nastiness is a defence mechanism meant to keep the world at a distance, I have to tell you it works.'

A look of complete astonishment replaced the sneer. Then he threw her totally. The grin that revealed his even white teeth and some gorgeous crinkly lines around his eyes also ironed out the engrained lines of cynicism around his mouth.

The breath snagged in her throat as she stared at the transformation. *Mercy, he's gorgeous!*

Then he completed the transformation by throwing back his head and laughing. The uninhibited sound was deep, warm and attractive.

'You have quite a tongue on you.'

There was no mistaking the reluctant admiration in his voice. Sam found it more disturbing than his hostility. Brows knitted in consternation, she backed out of the door, unaware until she was in the open air that she had been holding her breath.

CHAPTER FIVE

THE first spatters of rain were falling from the already darkening sky as Sam ran towards the Land Rover to get the first-aid kit. She hoped the storm would hold off until she got back to Home Farm. A childhood incident had left her with an irrational fear of thunder, and heavy rain made the road back with its hairpin bends and dramatic drops a nightmare.

She was briefly tempted to get in and drive away, and delegate the task of helping this ungrateful man to someone else. But not going back in would have been admitting she was afraid of feeling whatever it was this stranger had churned up.

The kitchen, with its inglenook fireplace and flagged floor, was as big as a barn, but despite this Sam felt as if the stone walls were closing in on her as she stepped back inside. The stranger had a way of making any space seem confined.

'Would you like to sit down?' she asked. It was an invitation that Sam wouldn't have minded accepting herself—her knees had the consistency of cotton wool as she approached him.

His expression was surly as he held out his arm towards her, peeled off the towel and snapped, '*Dio mio*, woman, just get on with it if you must.'

'Is this the Italian charm I've heard so much about?' Her voice faded when she saw the edges of the gaping wound he had exposed on his palm. 'You really need to see a doctor. It might need suturing…'

'What I need is peace and quiet, so either put on a Band-Aid or go.'

Sam sighed reading the note of finality of his pronouncement. She didn't have to be psychic to see he wasn't a man who would recognise compromise if it hit him on his rather perfect nose.

She took his wrist and held his hand over the Belfast sink as she cleaned the area with antiseptic from the first-aid kit.

He accepted her ministrations in silence punctuated only by the rain that began to lash against the window.

The storm and the heaviness in the air probably accounted for ninety per cent of the weird tension that held her in its grip.

'The storm is coming.'

Almost before the words were out of her mouth lightning flashed, filling the room with white. Sam tensed.

The storm was here.

'What's wrong?'

'Nothing…lightning. I'm not keen on storms.' In the distance Sam could hear the dull roll of thunder and he obviously did too.

'It's quite close.'

'I'd worked that out for myself,' she said crankily, keeping her head bent over his hand. 'Sorry if this is hurting.' She attached the final strip of tape to the bandage. 'Done.' She angled a questioning look at his face. She was pretty sure what his response would be, but she felt obliged to ask anyway. 'Would you like me to call someone for you?'

'I would like—'

At that moment there was a bang so loud that Sam shrieked and leapt as though shot. She saw the contents of the first-aid box hit the floor and a second later she couldn't see anything at all—the lights went out and the room was plunged into inky darkness.

'Calm down, woman, it's only a bit of thunder.'

Despite the irritation in his voice she supposed the hand that fell on her shoulder was meant to offer comfort.

'The lights have gone out,' she said.

His face had separated itself out from the darkness, a more solid shadow, but she could not make out any details of his features as he responded in a voice wiped clean of all expression.

'They went out for me five weeks ago.'

Only five weeks! Her eyes widened in shock and for a moment she was not conscious of the storm.

'Was it gradual or…?'

The fingers on her arm tightened. 'You mean did I have time to practise with my white cane and learn Braille? No, I didn't. It was the side effect of surgery following an accident. But let's look on the bright side—I'm the man you want around when the lights go out. And are you scared of the dark, my ministering angel?'

'Are you?' She reached out for his face, trailing her fingers down strong contours, trying to translate the tactile messages into an image…was this how he saw?

Did he live with a fear of the blackness he now faced every day? The thought of his dark world made something twist hard inside Sam. She reached up and grabbed his head, drawing his mouth to hers and pressing her lips against his. She kissed him with a ferocity born of, not just lust, but sharp, sweet tenderness.

He did not react. There was the space of several heartbeats, during which she wanted the floor to open up and swallow her, before he responded, kissing her back with the wild desperation of a starving man.

'Sometimes,' she heard herself admit when the kiss ended and she was standing there shaking, 'I'm scared of just about everything.' But nothing in her life so far made her as scared as the rush of primal need she felt in the arms of this total stranger.

'You hide it well.'

She couldn't hide her response when his hand slid under her top, his long fingers skating over the hot skin of her back. She didn't actually try.

And when he bent his dark head and fitted his mouth to hers, parting her lips with his tongue, she met it with her own. As his mouth lifted a fractured moan escaped past the emotional thickening in Sam's aching throat. Then she could feel his breath warm against her neck, stirring the downy hairs on her cheek as he took her face between his hands and ran his thumbs across the trembling outline of her lips, swollen from his hungry kisses.

'*Dio Mio*, it's been a long time,' he slurred thickly.

Sam was shaking inside and out as she whispered, 'You've not lost the knack, I promise you.'

He ran his tongue slowly along the curve of her upper lip, a slow sensual smile forming on his own mouth when his actions drew a second deep throaty moan from her. 'I haven't wanted a woman for a long time.'

His words sent a fresh rush of heat through her body. 'But you want me?'

The electricity in the lengthening silence had nothing to do with the storm raging outside. When he finally spoke his voice was thick and heavily accented.

'What do you think?' His big hands slid to her hips and, cupping her bottom, he drew her hard against his body so that she could feel the strength of his arousal.

A whimpering sound left her throat as she felt the erotic imprint of his erection in the soft flesh of her belly.

'Will you take all of me, *cara*?' Without waiting for a response he took hold of the hem of her top, and peeling it over her head, flung it over his shoulder before reaching for the clip on her bra.

A tiny sliver of sense surfaced and Sam shook her head.

'Not yet.'

Shivering as the cool air hit her overheated skin, Sam was glad of the dark as he suggested, 'For you too, I think, it has been a long time?' His voice shook, tremors raking his lean frame as he bent his head and claimed her lips again.

Sam was startled when, his hands still anchored to her hips, he fell to his knees. He placed a hand in the small of her back and drew her towards him.

'What are you…?' She broke off, gasping as she felt the flicker of his tongue across her hardened nipples through the silk of her bra. Her head went back and a low keening cry left her throat as the erotic caress sent a pulse of heat deep into her pelvis, then again and again as he drew the tight peak into his mouth.

'Oh, God!' she moaned, and didn't recognise her voice. Her head was spinning and she couldn't focus. Her body was on fire; every nerve ending was screaming for his attention. Her knees sagged and she thought how she couldn't take any more of what he was doing, except maybe the words were not in her head, maybe she said them out loud, because he groaned.

'Me neither, *cara*.' Then he picked her up, his big hands cupped under her bottom supporting her weight as he rose to his feet in fluid motion.

Feet clear of the ground, Sam linked her arms behind his head and kissed him hard on his mouth. He tasted of whisky and she remembered the empty bottles.

'Are you drunk?'

'That would be an excuse,' he agreed. 'But, no, I'm not, though neither do I think I am totally sane.' He bent his head to kiss her once more.

'You taste so good,' he slurred thickly. 'Do all ministering angels taste this good?'

'Don't stop!' she pleaded, her fingers tangling in his hair drawing his face to her body.

'I won't...I can't.' Something in his voice conveyed he found the situation incomprehensible, which made two of them, Sam thought, clinging on tight as in total pitch darkness he took the flight of stone stairs two a time. He acted as though she weighed nothing. The muscles in his arms, and for that matter everywhere else, were obviously not just for show.

He kicked open the bedroom door and backed in carrying her. A flash of lightning zigzagged in the sky outside the stone mullion and for a moment she saw the room and him.

By the time he laid her on the four-poster and joined her the darkness had closed back in around them like a blanket, but the memory of the primal need etched into his dark features stayed with her.

She felt his hands on her body stripping off her remaining clothes, his touch adding fuel to the fire of frustration that was growing inside her.

She could hear his breath come faster as he touched her breasts, weighing and cupping them in his hands—by which time she was not breathing at all.

As his hands slid down her body she recalled reading somewhere that a person's inhibitions were freed in the dark. It had to be true because now she found herself taking his hand and pressing it against the damp apex of her legs, urging him to touch her.

'This isn't me,' she whispered as he slid fingers into her heat and dampness, causing her body to arch like a bow. She was on fire, she was melting…she was aching.

'Well, whoever you are, *cara*, you're the best thing that has happened to me in a long time.'

She let out a cry of protest when he levered himself off her, but literally seconds later he returned and his clothes were gone. The skin-to-skin contact sent a shock wave through her body, but it also seemed to kick-start her natural instincts into life.

'You're beautiful!' She felt her first rush of feminine power as she laid a hand flat on his chest and a ripple shuddered through his body. 'God, you feel so good.'

It was liberating and wildly exciting to slide her fingers over his smooth skin and hear his harsh intake of breath as her fingers tangled in the hair on his chest before sliding lower. The rippling male strength of his body fascinated her.

Her eyes closed tight, her breath coming in tiny gusty puffs, she let her hand trail even lower.

Her gasp and hasty withdrawal soon afterwards drew a low husky chuckle from the man beside her.

'I said it had been a long time.' He kissed her mouth and breathed thickly. 'It's what you do to me.'

Adjusting his position so that they lay face to face, he pulled her leg across his hip. He let her feel his arousal against her belly, then drew her hand down between them, curling her fingers around the hard shaft.

A flash of heat washed over her body as things shifted and tightened low in her pelvis. 'You are incredible…'

This time it was Cesare who pulled her hand away, stifling her small cry of protest with his mouth. As they kissed with a feverish desperation their bodies pressed into one another as they fought to be one.

The anticipation lodged like a fist behind her breastbone as he flipped her onto her back. He was a dark shadow above her as he laid a hand either side of her head.

A fractured sigh left her lips as he inserted a knee between her legs and opened them before settling between them. As he thrust up and into her a shocked cry was wrenched from Sam's throat at the moment of intimate invasion.

Above her she was conscious of him speaking in the same tone as someone might use to gentle a scared animal. His voice was low, and he might have been saying anything—she didn't understand a word of Italian—but it sounded incredible. He also felt incredible and while she sort of knew what came next she couldn't wait to find out.

She grabbed his shoulders, sliding her fingers down the smooth contours of his muscled back until they came to rest on his taut buttocks.

Above her she could hear the harsh sound of his laboured breathing. She grabbed really hard, arched against him and begged, 'Please!'

The fierce request drew a groan from his chest. 'Don't push too hard. I need to stay in control…'

Sam didn't need him in control, she needed him out of control. The fire in her blood was telling her she did.

He seemed to get the drift of her fierce request because a moment later he responded, and started to move, building a steady rhythm as he thrust deeper and deeper into her.

Her body closed around him and she wrapped her legs around his waist as the raw urgency that boiled in her blood took her over completely.

The anticipation built inside her until she thought she might explode or ignite—she did both.

It started slowly with small quivers and then it

hit her, the strength of the climatic moment shocking a cry from her lips as she felt his hot release inside her.

He lay on top of her, neither making any effort to break the intimate connection until he groaned, 'I'll crush you, *cara*,' and rolled off her.

Sam, who had liked being crushed by his heavy male body, lay there not knowing what to do until he suddenly reached out and pulled her into his side.

'You'll get cold over there, angel.' He pulled the cover up over her and pulled her head onto his chest. 'Sorry, I haven't slept in days, but I will now. Don't go anywhere.'

As she lay in his arms and listened to him breathing deep and steady she remembered overhearing a friend say something after she had just ended a particularly turbulent relationship.

'Sex is not the cure, it's the drug and it's often worse than the disease that was there to begin with. It's better to be lonely than need anyone that much.'

It had not made sense to Sam at the time, but now it did. She hadn't felt lonely before, she

hadn't felt her life was missing any vital ingre-
dient, but now she did.

She lifted her chin. She was a grown-up; she
was going to move on; she wasn't going to have
her life defined by one chance meeting—and
one deeply flawed, charismatic, fascinating man.

But there seemed no point moving on until the
storm did the same.

Now, twelve weeks later, Sam could marvel at
her naivety when she had thought moving on
would be that simple. One experience had taught
her that it was easier said than done especially
when she had a constant reminder of that man
and that night.

She sighed, pressed a hand to her stomach and
thought of how much she would love this baby,
no matter what.

'I said, lady, you might as well get out and walk
from here. This traffic is not going to move.'

Sam looked at the taxi driver, her blank gaze
slowly clearing from her face. 'Th-thank you,'
she stuttered, reaching in her bag for her purse.

The ability of the past to drag her back in this

way was something she had to resist. It was totally pointless to revisit it and a mistake to assume any closeness to the man because they had shared one night.

She might have lain in his arms and laid her head to his heart while he slept, but he remained a total enigma. She still didn't have a clue what went on in his head, but maybe that was for the best. They belonged in different worlds.

She told herself she was glad that he had rejected the chance to take any role in his child's life. At least that meant she could keep him out of hers and out of her head too, she decided, pinning on a bright upbeat smile.

'Keep the change,' she said to the taxi driver as she handed him some money before vanishing into the mass of other pedestrians. Today had been a big mistake, but she was over it, and him, already.

CHAPTER SIX

SAM glanced at her watch before she knocked on the door of the editor's office—damn!

It was ten minutes after the time Eric Gibbs had said he wanted her to meet him. Eric was well known for two things: his beard, which made him look like an avuncular Father Christmas, and his almost paranoid aversion to being kept waiting by anyone.

He had been known to walk out on Hollywood royalty because they were late and she wasn't a famous actor or a diva, she was a very junior journalist whose temporary contract was just coming to an end.

It was a nail-biting place to be for anyone who had her share of insecurities—which Sam did.

A few weeks earlier being offered this contract had been the focus of all her ambitions, and the possibility that the man himself might be about to offer it to her would have had her in a state of feverish anticipation.

Now, when financial security mattered more than ever, Sam knocked on the door feeling oddly detached.

The chances were this was nothing to do with her contract at all. Eric Gibbs had more important items on his agenda than the contracts of very junior members of his staff. On the two occasions they had met face to face he had got her name wrong, though she'd been told not to take that personally. Apparently Eric was not good with names and called everyone from royalty to government ministers 'mate'.

But if it wasn't the contract what else could explain this abrupt summons on her day off? She might have had more of a clue if her mental discipline hadn't disintegrated. She couldn't string two thoughts together without Cesare muscling his way into her head.

'Get over him, Sam!' she counselled herself sternly. If he didn't want anything to do with this baby, that was his loss. She frowned, lifted her chin and said 'His loss!' just as the office door opened. 'S-sorry,' she muttered, blushing to the roots of her hair.

'I said come in.'

'I didn't hear, I'm…'

'Never mind. Sit down…I'll get straight to the point.'

He did and Sam listened, the knot of anxiety in her stomach having grown into a gaping chasm by the time he had finished speaking.

'So you're sacking me?' It was a shock—more than a shock. She was insecure, but she was not delusional—she knew she was good.

The editor's direct gaze wandered in the direction of the potted plant on the filing cabinet. 'We have to let you go. Sorry and all that.'

Sam got to her feet struggling for dignity. It was hard when her knees were shaking so hard. 'Not as sorry as me.'

'Of course, we'll give you excellent references.'

'What have I done wrong?'

'This isn't about you, it's about… Damn them!' he growled, slamming his fist down on the desk causing a pile of papers to slide to the floor.

Sam watched the inexplicable display of anger, but it didn't have the power to touch her. She was numb.

'It's about organisational changes.'

Sam accepted the vague explanation with a shrug. 'I'll take my things with me, shall I?'

'No hurry...no hurry,' Eric said, looking awkward as he gave her shoulder a squeeze.

Sam managed to collect her things without bumping into anyone she knew. She was halfway home before the anger kicked in and she was articulate after the fact. A hundred things she knew she should have said—haughty, cutting things—popped into her head. By the time she reached her bedsit the anger had given way to misery, self-pity and tears that blinded her as she pushed the key into the door and let herself in.

She dropped the things she was holding onto the floor and flung herself headlong on the sofa.

They had been sitting in the stationary car for half an hour before Paolo, sitting in the driving seat, spoke up.

'There is a lady coming, petite, she has red hair and she's crying.'

The last comment was the clincher.

'She is going into the building.' The thickset Italian continued speaking in his native tongue.

'We will follow her,' Cesare said, trying not to think about the tears. This was a situation where the ends definitely justified the means.

Paolo responded with an affirmative grunt, but expressed no surprise at the announcement. He had worked for Cesare for ten years and the role required flexibility. He waited until Cesare had slid from the back seat and then placed a light guiding hand unobtrusively on his employer's elbow as they walked towards the building the woman had gone into.

'It is the fifth floor, flat 17b.'

Was she weeping in flat 17b?

Cesare's expression hardened into a mask of resolution as he continued to refuse to ac-knowledge his guilt, and the part he had played in her tears.

'The lift is out of order, sir,' Paolo said in a tone that suggested this did not surprise him.

'The building does not meet with your approval? It could do with a lick of paint?' Cesare speculated.

'Several. Or, better still, knocking down.'

Cesare laughed. 'You are a snob.' Then his expression sobered. A building that his fastidious driver found unacceptable was not one that he had any intention of his child being raised in.

The thickset Paolo, who carried a few extra pounds around his middle, was panting by the time they reached the fourth floor. Cesare was not.

'You need to take more exercise, my friend.'

Paolo acknowledged the comment with a grunt before giving his employer a rapid thumbnail sketch of their surroundings. He knew that his employer's remarkably retentive memory would not require him to repeat himself.

'You wish me to wait?'

'No. I will call when I need you.'

Sam was still lying on the sofa wearing her damp coat when the doorbell began to ring. It was only when the man from the flat upstairs began banging on the floor and it became obvious that her visitor was not going to go away that she made any attempt to respond.

'All right, all right,' she muttered, running the back of her hand across her damp cheeks and glancing with disinterest in the mirror as she passed. The glance revealed a blotchy, tear-stained face and swollen eyes surrounded by a halo of wild, slightly damp red curls.

Sniffing and pushing her hair back from her face, she opened the door a crack, but before she could either tell her noisy visitor to go away or even just check them out the door was thrust open and she was lifted backwards into her cramped hallway as Cesare Brunelli's broad-shouldered, six-foot-five frame entered her flat.

For thirty seconds she was too stunned to say or do anything at all.

As his hands fell from her waist Cesare was unable to dispel the illogical feeling that they had belonged there—they fitted. Shrugging off the whimsical idea, he drew a hand through his hair and it came away wet. It had been raining outside.

'Say something or I will start to think I have wandered into the wrong flat.'

It was a lie. He could have picked out her subtle womanly fragrance in a room crammed with hundreds of bodies, and he didn't think this had anything to do with some sensory compensation he had developed. His sixth sense had not come out of hibernation, but there was, it seemed, just something about her that he reacted to on an almost cellular level.

The mass of raw masculinity in such an enclosed space sent Sam's nervous system and her brain into chaotic confusion. She expelled a long shaky sigh as her wide-eyed glance slid down the long, lean length of him, a weakness invading her limbs as a deeper shuddery sigh left her with parted lips. He looked incredible—the epitome of male beauty standing close enough for her to touch. Only she wasn't going to—she still had a grain of good sense left and past experience had taught her that when any form of physical contact with the Italian took place things got dangerously unpredictable.

She stared covetously at him and wondered what to do next—the question might be academic if her heart beat any faster. The moleskin jacket he wore hung open to reveal a close-fitting cashmere sweater, black, like the jeans that emphasised his long, muscular thighs and snaky hips.

She tried to drag her eyes away but couldn't stop staring. There was a sheen of moisture on his golden skin making it gleam, and the same moisture clung in silvery droplets to the long eyelashes that framed his beautiful eyes.

He had not hidden them behind dark glasses, but then Cesare Brunelli was not a hiding sort of man. He was more of a hit-obstacles-head-on sort of person.

She suspected that most things moved—or even ran—when they saw him coming! If she had shown as much sense, she reflected bitterly, she wouldn't be in this mess. Although she supposed she would still be out of work, only it would be because she hadn't made the grade, which wasn't as bad as out of work because she hadn't made the grade and was pregnant!

She finally managed to speak. 'You didn't wander in, you barged in uninvited.' She tried hard to inject the necessary degree of coldness and disapproval into her voice, but it was an uphill battle because it was hard to be cold when she was staring at his mouth. 'How did you get here?' She started at the sound of the door being closed with an audible click. 'And what are you doing here?'

Hearing the rising note of escalating panic in her voice, she stopped and cleared her throat.

'Actually this is a bad time for m-me…'

The husky catch in her voice had a similar effect on Cesare as a nerve ending being exposed to cold air. His brows drew together in a stern line as his forehead puckered into a frown. 'You're crying!'

Scalding shame washed over him. He firmed his jaw, causing the muscles along the strong angular outline to quiver. This was not the place for sentiment; he was doing the right thing. It was necessary.

Sam sniffed and placed both hands across her mouth to muffle the sob she felt welling up in her throat.

'Will you just go away?' she pleaded.

'No, I couldn't if I wanted to.' He passed a

hand across his eyes and smiled sardonically. 'I'm blind, remember.'

'I remember.' It was still hard to believe, even more so now that he had conquered the demons of primitive fear he had been wrestling in Scotland. Did he resent the fact she had seen him when he was not totally in control?

'In case you didn't recognise it, that was black humour.'

'No, that was bad taste.'

'I'm famous for it.'

Sam couldn't respond to the quip; her facial muscles felt locked in a tragic expression. 'Look…' She paused, wondering what to call him. She couldn't call the father of her child *Mister*! 'Look, Cesare—'

Some emotion she could not interpret flickered at the backs of his eyes. 'Was that so hard?' he asked.

Her eyes widened. Even though he couldn't pick up on the cues of body language and facial expressions everyone took for granted, he was scarily perceptive.

'Was what so hard?'

'Saying my name.'

She was too emotionally whacked to prevaricate. 'Yes, it was.' And why not? Anything connected with him was hard work!

'Cesare, the fact is I've had a bad day. The last person in the world I want to see is you!' Unable to stop them, she felt the tears start to roll down her cheeks once more and she wiped them away with the back of her hand.

'Sometimes it helps to talk about it.'

'For goodness' sake, don't turn kind and understanding now—not unless you want me to cry all over you, and that isn't a pretty sight,' she warned him darkly.

Cesare, who was well aware that even the most generous of critics could not have termed his recent actions either kind or understanding, reached out and touched the side of her cheek. She twisted her head away, but not before the shiver that ran through her body communicated itself to him through his fingertips.

'The advantage of being in the company of a blind man, *cara*, is you can relax about the way you look and not worry about bad-hair days.'

He might not be able to see her face or read her body language, but Sam recognised with a sense of dismay that she felt more exposed on every level when she was near him.

'I could *never* relax in your company.' She bit her quivering lips and added before he could read something revealing into her retort, 'I tried to talk to you…Cesare, and all it got me was a headache. Look, I'm sorry. I know you were only trying to do the right thing by suggesting we get married…you're Italian and the family thing is…'

She stopped as her shoulders began to shake with the effort of biting back the sobs that were locked in her throat. Her head sank to her chest as she began to sob in earnest.

Her muffled cries tore at Cesare's heart the way no woman's tears ever had.

He took a step forward and walked into an unseen obstacle. Stepping over it with a curse, he extended his hands and felt the silky top of her head. She lifted it and his hands slid to frame it. He moved a thumb across the wetness of her cheeks.

She sniffed and covered his hands with her own, but, instead of pulling them away, they stayed there holding his in place. 'Sorry, this isn't about you. I have to focus.'

Cesare told himself the same thing a hundred times a day—he had to focus and stay in control. When he spoke he did so from experience—he knew that ignoring feelings did not make them go away. 'No, you need to let go.' She had been there when he had let go and had taken the full brunt of his rage when he had.

The rest of his sentence remained unsaid as she suddenly walked into his arms, burrowed her wet face into his chest and said in a voice muffled by his sweater, 'I *need* you to shut up and hold me.'

For a second Cesare didn't react at all to the imperious command. Inner conflict was tearing him apart, which made no sense—there was only conflict when someone wasn't sure they had done the right thing, and Cesare, not a man afflicted with self-doubt, was sure.

He had been able to view the situation with total objectivity. The ability to have a clear overview without getting bogged down with emotional irrelevancies combined with luck was a talent that had helped make him a very wealthy man. He was discovering that it wasn't easy to retain a grip on that objectivity when his arms were filled with a soft, weeping woman. Her scent flooded his senses and his arms closed around her.

Feelings, strong and unfamiliar, stirred as he stroked her hair and felt her quivering body relax. He slid the bulky wet coat she wore off her shoulders and moved his hands in a soothing motion down her spine. Then he propped his chin against the top of her glossy head and tried to keep things in perspective.

There would be other jobs.

But that wasn't the point and Cesare knew it. He had known it when he had rung the proprietor of the *Chronicle* and called in a favour, but he had rationalised his actions—that was harder now when he was seeing the consequences up close and personal.

Very close!

Her curves slotted into his angles as if they had been made to complement each other. He tried to think about why he was doing this, but thoughts of having her soft and warm under-neath him kept intruding.

He had been angry and in shock; his pride had been hurt when she had called him second best. He was still assailed by a need to hear her retract that statement, an odd desire for a man who had never given a damn for anyone's opinion of him.

What she thought of him was not relevant, though he would clearly be more comfortable married to someone who didn't hate his guts.

They must be married.

His immediate move after she had left his offices had been to cancel his trip back to Italy the next morning. His next had been the call to Mark James to call in a favour. The man had not been entirely happy at the request to interfere with what was, he pointed out, a purely editorial decision, but he had obliged anyway.

Samantha would not be offered a contract.

It seemed reasonable to Cesare to assume that being without a job would make the fiercely in-dependent Samantha appreciate the insecurity of her position. She would be in a more favourable frame of mind to consider his proposal, or at least not dismiss it out of hand.

The irony was not lost on Cesare. He had spent his entire adult life escaping the clutches of women with designs on him—or at least his money—and now he was being forced to employ deception and dirty tactics in order to sell himself as a good marriage bargain.

Cesare had pushed aside any disquiet he felt about employing such methods; he would do anything to ensure that, unlike himself, his child would not be brought up without a father. That his child would never feel as though he didn't belong. Parents wanted for their children the things they had been deprived of and he was no exception.

While she gave vent to her pent-up emotions Sam was unaware of anything but the shelter and security Cesare's arms offered. She ought to have pulled away the second she became aware of anything else, like the heat and hardness of his body and the male, clean, musky scent of his skin, but she didn't. She stayed there, her eyes tight shut, wanting the moment to last.

Cesare was the cause of, not the solution to, her problems, which made the fact she felt safe for the first time in weeks in his arms all the more bizarre.

She was losing it, she told herself.

Hands flat against his chest, she pushed away.

There was an awkward silence.

'S-sorry about that. You were in the wrong place at the wrong time, I'm afraid.'

He arched a brow, the roughness in his deep voice masking the emotions he felt hearing the catch in her voice. 'Things will look better in the morning—is that what they say?'

'Not in this case. I lost my job today.' Why was she telling him this?

Without waiting for him to respond, she walked into the sitting room and took up a cross-legged posture on an armchair. When she looked up she saw he had followed her and was feeling his way along the wall.

For a moment she was lost in admiration and awe for the way he had adapted. She could imagine nothing more terrifying than walking into somewhere strange and not having a clue of where she was. Yet he betrayed no hesitation. His dominating presence radiated confidence and immediately made the small room feel a lot smaller.

There was no doubt Cesare Brunelli was a very remarkable man—even if he was extremely aggravating.

'There's a chair just to your left.'

Cesare accepted the information with a nod and felt for the chair before he lowered himself into it.

'Why did you lose your job?'

'It turns out I'm not as good at what I was doing as I thought. Do you dislike bad journalists less than competent ones?'

He frowned. 'Is that what they said? That you were…'

'Hopeless.' She shrugged and stared at her fingers clenched in her lap. 'Not directly,' she admitted with a twisted smile. 'But it's fairly obvious.' A person had to accept facts even when they were unpalatable.

Cesare was annoyed by the flat acceptance in her voice. He had manipulated the situation, he had wanted her to feel vulnerable—just not this vulnerable. She was a fighter; she'd been fighting since the moment they had met! Somehow it felt wrong to him to hear her sound so resigned and defeated.

'So you're going to give up.'

Sam lifted her head, the anger she had heard in his voice, the anger she assumed was aimed at her, etched in the taut lines of his face.

'I didn't have you down as a defeatist,' he added.

His harsh contempt stung. 'I'm not, I'm a realist.' She glared at him and realised she still had no idea why he was here.

She supposed it had something to do with the baby, but what? Her eyes widened then narrowed as an unpleasant suspicion took hold; her hands clenched, her heart felt heavy and cold like ice in her chest. If he dared suggest she get rid of the baby…

'What will you do? Stay with your parents?'

'Dad died when I was ten, Mum died last year.'

'I'm sorry.'

There was caution in her expression as she searched his face. His sympathy seemed genuine. His mouth distracted her as it always did. She felt a stab of guilt and tore her eyes away. Staring that way when he couldn't see felt like an intrusion. She was invading his privacy like some sort of voyeur.

She gave a little noncommittal grunt and added, 'It wasn't totally unexpected—she'd lived with illness for years. She'd been in remission before and beat it when it came back, but last time...' emotion clogged in her throat as she struggled to keep her voice level '...she didn't.'

The prosaic little sniff made something tighten in Cesare's chest. He could not see her face but he *knew* she was frowning, terrified that he would think she was courting his sympathy.

How did he know that?

'Are your parents alive?'

'Very much so.'

'I suppose you're worried about what they will think about the baby.'

'They are busy with their own lives.' His father had discovered the joys of parenthood the previous year when he turned sixty. His new wife was twenty-two. His mother's attention was focused on his teenage half-sisters and keeping herself youthful looking for her husband—she had never admitted to the cosmetic surgery but the lines kept magically disappearing.

'Will you tell them?' As Sam asked the question she wondered whether he was thinking there would be no need if he persuaded her to terminate the pregnancy.

Cesare smoothly steered away from the subject of his family. 'So what are your plans, then?'

'Look for a new job.' She glared at him and thought, *And keep my baby*. 'I need to pay the rent. You never know, my experience as a cleaner might be useful. I might come to you for a reference.'

She watched his lips curl into a smile and knew he was going to say something that she wouldn't like—or maybe like too much? Her problem was her reactions to Cesare were so incompatible with the common sense everyone said she possessed.

His voice dropped an octave as he observed smokily, 'The talents I could verify might not get you the sort of job you're after, *cara*.'

She knew he was trying to insult her, not seduce her, so the thrill of excitement that made her stomach muscles quiver was all the more inexplicable.

'If all you can do is make snide, sarky comments like that you might as well leave—you might as well leave anyway!' she yelled. 'Unless you have any better suggestions.' She blew her nose and tucked a stray strand of hair behind her ear as she fixed him with a suspicious stare.

'I do actually.'

Sam tensed. 'I'm listening…'

'Did you mean it yesterday?'

She eyed him warily. 'Mean what?'

'Mean me being blind had nothing to do with you knocking back my proposal.'

'Yes, it didn't.' He was probably relieved today that she had refused.

'Prove it.'

The challenge brought a furrow to her brow. 'How?'

'Say yes now.'

CHAPTER SEVEN

S<small>AM</small> jerked back in her seat as though someone had struck her.

'You still want me to marry you?' She gasped hoarsely.

Cesare gave a fluid shrug. 'Why not? You are carrying my child, Samantha. Nothing has changed except your ability to support yourself.' He angled an enquiring brow and tilted his head to one side in a listening attitude.

Sam would have given anything to tell him it didn't matter, that losing her job made no difference—but it did.

She glanced down at the hand laid against her still-flat belly. 'Do you think I don't know that?' She chewed absently on her lower lip and sighed. 'It's ironic, really—I thought for a second you might have been here to suggest...'

Sam stopped, very conscious that he was alert to every nuance in her voice. He seemed to possess the disturbing ability to hear not only *what* a person said, but also what they *didn't* say.

'You thought I was going to suggest what?'

The admission came out in a defiant rush. 'I thought you might not want me to go ahead with the pregnancy.'

He looked blank for a moment. 'Not...' Then he froze.

Sam watched the dark colour run up under his skin, deepening his naturally dark complexion and then receding, leaving him deadly pale.

With unwilling fascination she watched his chest lift as he struggled to contain the outrage that was written into every hard line of his expressive face.

When he finally spoke his low voice vibrated with the strength of his feelings. '*Dio Mio*, you thought that I would ask you to terminate the pregnancy?' He broke off and slid into a flood of extremely angry-sounding Italian.

Sam stubbornly struggled to cling to the shreds of her defiance in face of his display of incandescent rage. 'I can see how it would seem like a solution to you.' She winced, thinking that she sounded like a sulky, petulant child. Why, she despaired, did she always end up feeling as though she was at fault where he was concerned?

Cesare's nostrils flared as he sucked in a deep breath. It was nice to know what a high opinion she had of him. 'You see nothing, *cara*!' he ground from between clenched teeth. 'Except what you wish to see! I am the bad man in your story, but this is not a story and if it was it would not belong to you alone.'

'Very cryptic. Are you trying to make a point?' she challenged.

He inclined his dark head in a jerky motion. 'This is *our* story...*our* child. And a child needs two parents.'

'They generally have two. It isn't optional, unlike marriage.' She jumped to her feet to put some distance between them and began to pace the room angrily.

'There is no need to bounce around in that emotional way.'

'I'll be as emotional as I like,' she retorted.

'This marriage will be a paper arrangement...'

She cut across him shrilly. 'You're talking as if it is inevitable and, anyway, what are you talking about...paper arrangement?'

'Marriages do not have to be for ever.'

His own parents' marriage had not been. His father—a serial adulterer—had walked out on Cesare's tenth birthday and the contact with his absent parent during the rest of his childhood had been limited to Christmas cards and the odd birthday present—usually a month or so late.

Cesare was determined that his own son would never be the little boy inventing the marvellous trips his father had taken him on to friends who had full-time fathers. His mother had done her best, but once she had remarried her new family— including three younger half-sisters—had obviously been the main focus of her attention.

Cesare had never quite belonged.

Sam stopped within a foot of his chair and said wistfully, 'I'd rather thought my marriage would last the test of time. Of course a man who is willing to take on another man's child might not be so easy to find.'

Cesare was silent as the words sank in—another man bringing up his child. Another man sharing a bed with Samantha.

The pressure in his temples increased, the dull throb became a deafening pounding.

But there was no hint of fury in his voice when he responded coldly, 'I hardly think now is the moment to be emotional.' The need to get his point across was more important than recognising the hypocrisy of the criticism. 'I am offering you a practical solution. Life as a single parent is not a bed of roses.'

'I'm aware of that,' she snapped, angry because he had neatly tapped directly into the escalating anxieties that were giving her nightmares. She had no job, the rent on her flat was astronomical and the place was not suitable for a baby, let alone a small child. What Cesare was offering, as cold, clinical and unpalatable as it seemed, would solve all her immediate problems.

She was well aware that most women in her situation would not view being offered marriage by an eligible billionaire as a problem. She should be thinking of the baby as he was, not herself. It wasn't as if he wanted to be saddled with a wife, but he was prepared to make that sacrifice.

'You cannot support even yourself.'

She pushed aside her tortured reflections and threw him a humourless smile. 'I see you prescribe to the kick-them-when-they're-down school of thought.' On anyone else the dark line scoring the razor-edged angle of his incredible cheekbones might have been suggestive of embarrassment, but he wasn't anyone else and she seriously doubted if he stocked the sentiment. 'Thanks for the concern, Cesare,' she said, laying on the insincerity with a trowel. 'But I'll…we'll manage.' Even she could hear the note of hysterical uncertainty in her voice.

His lips curled as he directed a black stare of hauteur in her direction. 'I do not wish my child to *manage*. I wish my child to have a stable upbringing, a father….'

'And you think I don't.'

His dark lashes lowered, brushing his cheeks. 'A mother should put the needs of her child ahead of her own wishes.'

Sam gasped. 'That is low, Cesare, even for you.'

He looked irritated and ran a hand through his hair, causing it to stick up at the front. 'What do you expect? You won't listen to reason, you're too stubborn and idealistic and…*Dio mio*! Do you not realise how your life would change as a single parent? Job satisfaction would be very low on your list of priorities. You would be forced to take work that paid, but did not necessarily offer you the challenges you need.'

'Challenges,' she echoed bitterly. 'I don't need challenges, I need—'

'Security,' he finished for her smoothly.

'Well, if I'm short of cash I can always do a kiss and tell. I still have contacts. Just imagine,' she invited, 'what the tabloids would pay.'

Cesare leaned back in his chair and Sam was irritated to see that he didn't look too bothered by the idea of his name being splashed all over the tabloids. 'Is that a threat?' he asked in a conversational tone.

'Could be.'

'The trick with threats is to never make them if you have no intention of following through.'

She eyed him with intense dislike. 'You would be the expert on threats.'

He smiled. 'If I make one you can be sure that I will follow through.'

Sam lowered her eyes before the irony hit her. She was dodging the stare of a man who couldn't even see her! He could intimidate her, though, without even trying. And Sam had no problem believing he would follow through with any threats he made—none at all.

Cesare was a dangerous man—she had known that from the moment she saw him. Her problem was she had a sneaking suspicion that that was part of his attraction for her. He was the forbidden fruit and to her eternal shame she couldn't look at him without contemplating taking another bite out of him!

'You have an original way of proposing, I'll give you that.'

'You wish me to go down on one knee and declare undying love?'

The sarcasm caught Sam on a raw nerve she hadn't known she had and she covered her reaction with a display of flippancy. 'Why not? I could do with a good laugh.'

Cesare ignored her mumbled facetious retort and turned his head so that all she could see was the pure, perfect lines of his patrician profile. 'Laughing would not be out of the question. You are dwelling on the negative aspects of this marriage, but there are some more positive ones. Let us be serious for a moment.'

The suggestion filled Sam with deep foreboding.

'You are an ambitious woman. I could help you.'

'If I'm going to get anywhere it will be on my own merits!'

'So we will leave nepotism aside for one moment. Marriage to me would give you the luxury of being able to pick and choose your next career move—on your own merits—or, on the other hand, should you wish you could take time out and spend time with the baby. The point is the choice would be yours.'

'You're a good salesman,' she conceded, her expression abstracted as she dropped to her knees beside his chair. 'But the thing about pacts with the devil is that they sound terrific until you read the small print and then you realise you've signed your soul away. So what do you get out of it? Why marriage?'

'The devil—surely that is typecasting?'

Sam ignored the dry interruption. '*Surely* it would be a whole lot simpler to just make some financial provision for the baby?'

'Possibly,' he conceded. 'But the legal rights of a father when he is not married to his child's mother are, as I understand it, virtually non-existent, and I, *cara*, wish to have an equal say in how our child is raised.'

'So that's what this sudden desire to get married is about?' It was totally irrational to find his motivation hurtful. It wasn't as if she wanted him to love her or anything.

'Partly,' he admitted. 'It is not a bad thing either that with a wife in the background I will hopefully not attract those women who wish to hold my hand while I cross the road.'

'So that will be my job.'

'No, I don't think I'll change the present arrangement, Paolo does not want to marry me. Besides, I suspect you would be more likely to lead me under a bus.'

'Don't give me ideas,' she growled before she subsided into thoughtful silence. Although she could not seriously consider his crazy suggestion, she was starting to fully appreciate the vulnerability of her situation. Losing her job this way had served to emphasise the fact that she just couldn't take anything for granted.

What if anything happened to her?

What if she became ill or worse...? What would happen to her baby then?

There was always her brother and his wife, but the young couple were struggling financially themselves and the last thing they needed was her adding to their problems.

'What are you thinking?' Cesare probed as the silence stretched and he struggled to hide his growing impatience. It frustrated him that he could not see her face.

'You usually seem to know.' Sam chewed on her lower lip and thought that sometimes he knew what she was thinking before she did. 'Who is Paolo?'

'Paolo is my driver and sometimes bodyguard should the need arise.' Irritated by the diversion, Cesare added, 'We are not discussing Paolo.'

'And has it ever arisen?' Sam found the idea that Cesare would ever be in a position where he needed someone to watch his back alarming.

'Will you stop changing the subject?'

'I was interested.' She didn't add that anything about him interested her. It might give him the wrong idea—*or the right idea*?

'And I was thinking that if I'd not seen that article and I'd decided not to tell you about the baby and anything happened...'

'Happened?'

'Well, things do.' She heaved a sigh and studied the pattern on the rug beneath her knees as she settled back onto her heels with a frown. It was a depressing thought and not one she, as a natural optimist, thought about often, but she couldn't escape facts. Cesare's comments had simply brought worries she already had into sharper focus. 'People get run over and killed crossing the road every day of the week.'

The prosaic observation caused a bone-deep chill to settle over Cesare as his imagination provided flashing images of pools of blood on a road, a warm body growing cold and stiff... A choking sound dragged from some place deep inside him.

The strange noise sent a chill down Sam's spine and brought her head up with a snap. 'Are you all right?' she asked, deeply alarmed by the grey tinge to his normally vibrant skin. The Stygian blackness of his unseeing stare as he looked back at her suggested the things he was seeing in his head were not pretty.

'Oh, you're thinking the baby would have ended up in care,' she said, seizing on what she believed was the cause of his visible distress. 'Don't worry, my brother and his wife would never let that happen.'

'*Madre dio*, woman, will you focus and stop prattling?' He raised a hand to his head; the pressure in his skull had grown to an explosive level as the truth he had been trying hard to avoid stared back at him.

Sam's eyes flashed; she was offended by the snarling brusqueness of his tone. 'I suppose when you make a decision you draw up a chart, work out statistical probabilities, weigh up the pros and cons all very scientifically,' she retorted sarcastically.

'Actually I am a great believer in following my gut instinct.'

And Cesare's gut instinct was telling him right now to kiss her. Open her mouth and taste the sweetness that was on offer within.

He followed up the throaty statement so quickly that Sam had no hint of his intention until his fingers curled around her chin. She didn't think of resistance as he tilted her face to one side to allow himself full access to her mouth. She just thought, *Please—please kiss me!*

Then he did. His mouth was on hers and his lips were moving with slow, sensual expertise that raised the feverish temperature of her over-heated blood to a bubbling simmer.

He drew back fractionally, breathing hard—or was that her...? Sam struggled to separate herself from him, not just physically, but emo-tionally too, and failed.

Intense-sounding words of Italian fell harshly from his lips as he bent his head and kissed her again with a driving possessive hunger she felt all the way down to her toes. Like a firework display, desire exploded inside her, driving the last shred of resistance or sense to the farthest foggiest recesses of her lust-soaked brain.

The kiss ended and her heavy lids half lifted, a sigh of sheer longing snagging in her aching throat as she traced his lean dark face.

They were so close she could see the fine texture of his skin, the lines radiating from the corners of his eyes and bracketing his sensual mouth, the scar on his forehead that disappeared into his thick, glossily dark hairline.

She lifted a hand to trace the physical evidence of the accident that had robbed him cruelly of his sight. She felt as if a hand had reached into her chest, icy fingers tightening around her heart as she thought of him hurting, waking up alone and in the dark.

His long, tapering fingers skimmed her face, drawing it up to his as he breathed, 'Open your mouth for me, *cara*.'

And she did, a little growl vibrating in her throat as she drew herself up onto her knees and wrapped her arms around his neck. She met his tongue with her own, breathing in the scent of him, the taste of him as her breasts were crushed against the hardness of his chest and her fingers slid over muscles that were hard and perfectly formed.

It was Cesare who drew back so abruptly that Sam fell back, only just stopping herself from tumbling onto her bottom with her hands.

She stared at him, eyes round, her pupils still hugely dilated, panting as she tried to suck air into her lungs.

She was filled with shame. 'That was…that shouldn't have happened.'

'But you knew it would, we both knew it would…'

She opened her mouth to deny this ludicrous claim and stopped. She pulled herself up onto her heels and sighed.

Cesare spoke. 'You know, if we're going to keep on ripping each other's clothes off every time we're in the same room I think we should get married.'

Embarrassed colour flared in Sam's cheeks as she smoothed down her top. 'I have my clothes on,' she replied with dignity. And so did he, she thought as her glance drifted to the V of golden skin visible where the top button of his shirt was unfastened. Her stomach quivered.

'That situation can be changed.'

She sucked in an audible outraged breath, which seemed a bit crazy considering that he knew every inch of her body intimately… She tried not to think about how intimately. He was obviously of the same opinion as his rumble of laughter was wicked and warm.

'You're blushing, aren't you?'

Her eyes widened. 'How do you know?'

'You have a very eloquent range of gasps and I can feel the changes in your body temperature from here.' Without warning he reached out and placed his open hand against her chest. 'From here it is easier—I can feel your heart trying to beat its way out. It's ironic—I'm blind and I've never come across a woman who is easier to read than you. How do you go through life showing so much?'

Sam stared mesmerised at his fingers splayed against her breast and shook her head. Sometimes the truth was the worst thing to say and this was one of those times. She knew it yet still she said it.

'It's only with you.'

His eyes darkened as he rasped, 'Come here.'

Sam's heart was hammering so loud it blocked out everything else as without thinking she raised herself up on her knees and leaned in to him until their faces were almost touching.

His fingers speared deep into her bright hair as he inhaled the fragrance that came from the silky skein. 'This is a side to the arrangement which would be most pleasurable for us both, *cara*,' he husked, resting his nose beside hers.

'The kissing…?'

His expression was solemn but his eyes fierce as he explained, 'Obligatory for married people.' He kissed the side of her mouth before dropping his head to trail a line of delicious damp kisses down her neck.

'Oh, God!' she groaned. 'I don't know why you can do this to me.'

'That makes two of us, but who cares?'

Sam couldn't approve of this reckless attitude and she said so, but he didn't seem to take her seriously—possibly because she was already unfastening the buttons of his shirt with shaking but determined fingers.

A deep sigh of pleasure escaped her throat as the material parted and his gleaming torso was revealed to her greedy gaze. 'You are just so beautiful… What?' she asked suddenly in hoarse protest as he grabbed both her wrists and lifted her hands from his warm skin.

'Marry me, Samantha.'

Her disbelief was tinged with indignation. 'Are you trying to blackmail me?'

'You mean will I withhold my favours if you don't say I do?' He laughed, but underneath the laughter the tension that pulled the skin taut against the magnificent bone structure of his face was visible. 'Good idea, *cara*,' he admitted. 'Only one problem—I'm really not endowed with that sort of self-denial.' Not where she was concerned anyway.

'I don't even like you,' she whispered against his mouth.

'Liking has nothing to do with it,' he rasped, tracing the shape of her full upper lip with his tongue before sliding it deep inside her mouth. A groan was wrenched from Sam's chest as she opened her mouth to increase the sensual penetration. 'Why fight it?'

Sam wasn't. Fighting was the very last thing she wanted to do. 'Is this supposed to be the clincher? You think you can kiss me into agreeing to marry you? Cesare, you're really not that good.'

But he was!

She found her fingers in his hair and kissed him on the mouth, the pent-up hunger she had been carrying around for weeks finding some release, but not enough.

'There are more powerful, primitive instincts at work here. We have a sexual connection.'

'I don't want a sexual connection!' she wailed.

His lips curved into a fleeting smile, but his expression remained intent as, with his heavy lids half closed, his fingers slid under her top.

'But you do want this, don't you?' he slurred, lifting the cotton top she wore and skating lightly across the smooth skin of her midriff before moving to cup one breast through the thin light lace covering of her bra. His thumb moved across her nipple; the seductive motion of his lips on her neck made her head spin. She felt on fire, out of control and loved it.

She watched him as he peeled the top over her head and flung it to one side.

He bent his head and, with one arm wrapped around her narrow ribcage, applied his mouth first to one straining breast, pulling the nipple into his mouth, and then administering the same exquisite torture to the other. Sam clung to him, her fingers digging into the muscles of his shoulders as her head fell back.

Fingers splayed across her spine, he brought her upright until their faces were almost touching. There was a fine mist of sweat over his skin and he was breathing as hard as she was. 'Marry me,' he said thickly.

CHAPTER EIGHT

SAM lifted a hand and ran it down the hard curve of Cesare's jaw.

'Couldn't we just go to bed?' she suggested hopefully.

One corner of his mouth lifted in a wolfish smile as he ran a finger slowly down the curve of her cheek. 'You're offering me some sympathy sex, *cara*?'

'I'm offering you me.'

He gasped, and she could feel a shudder run through his hard lean frame.

'I don't seem to have any pride where you're concerned. I'm utterly shameless.' She had never imagined that she could surrender herself so unconditionally to any man, let alone a man like Cesare.

She was totally unselfconscious but at the same

time more aware of her femininity than she had ever been in her life. Everything about this man was a contradiction and so were her feelings for him. The antagonism and attraction she felt for him bled into one confusing, powerful, all-consuming entity.

'You're utterly delicious,' he contradicted thickly. 'I have been thinking about being inside you.'

The erotic image his words created in her head made the ache low in her pelvis intensify. She stared into his eyes, she saw her reflection, saw the predatory glow and felt an equally primal response clutch like a tight fist deep inside her. Reckless desire tugged like a silken thread at Sam's senses as she watched her bra go the same way as her top. She shivered as the cool air touched her overheated skin.

'Then do it,' she whispered.

'Marry me.'

'Will you stop saying that? People don't make decisions just like that,' she protested, pressing her lips to his throat and tasting the salt of his skin.

'Forget people. We're not people, we're us. We made a baby, Samantha. *He* needs us.'

He made a compelling argument. Feelings

struggled and warred inside her; her sex-soaked brain wouldn't work. On one level what he was saying made sense and it was attractive, on another it terrified her witless!

'What about me? Doesn't it matter what I need?'

'You need me.' And right now he needed her. The hunger roared in his blood like a furnace, drowning out the nagging edge of guilt over his manipulation of the situation.

'A paper arrangement, you said?'

A slow smile of male triumph spread across his face. 'We'll talk about it later. Right now I think we should finish this in the comfort of a bed. You do have a bed?'

'Yes, I have a bed.'

He fitted his hand in hers. 'Then lead the way, *cara*,' he said, rising to his feet and pulling her with him.

'I didn't say yes.'

'Of course you did,' he said with smug male complacence before he kissed her and made her feel as though she'd say anything he wanted her to.

* * *

It was two days later that Cesare accompanied her on her visit for her first scan.

The plush offices of the Harley Street clinic were a million miles from the NHS department she had expected to be attending.

Watching her budget was too deeply ingrained in Sam for her not to feel a flicker of guilt at her luxurious surroundings, but, having seen Cesare's expression when he'd spoken of the safety and health of his unborn child, she had recognised that this was not a point that he was prepared to be flexible on. It seemed better to save her energy for battles she could win.

Besides, she couldn't see Cesare standing pa-tiently in an NHS-clinic queue—he would probably behave so badly they would be asked to leave.

'What are you smiling at?'

Sam turned her head, astonished. 'How do you know I'm smiling?'

He shook his head, looked briefly perplexed by the question himself, and said, 'But you are?'

'I was thinking about you behaving badly.'

His voice dropped to the seductive purr that

always made her stomach muscles quiver. 'I thought you liked it when I behaved badly, *cara*?' he observed with a pretty feeble display of innocent surprise.

'I wasn't thinking of the bedroom.'

His grin deepened. 'I rarely think of any place else.' He didn't need to be psychic then to know she was blushing.

A few minutes later Sam knew Cesare's thoughts were not in the bedroom.

She turned her face briefly from the screen and the look she caught on his face tore at her heart. She had been too excited and enthralled by what she had seen to give a thought to how Cesare would feel hearing the doctor describing the images of their baby—images he could not see of a child he would never see.

Swept away on a wave of painful empathy, she caught his big strong hand between two of hers, for once not caring of his ultra sensitivity to any form of sympathy. To hell with his pride! His skin felt cold as she brought his hand to her chest; she felt the raw pain in his face as a physical ache.

Her expression grew determined. She could not make him see but she could share.

'You can see his head and his heart beating and that…' She threw a questioning glance towards the medic. 'The spinal cord?'

Cesare swallowed, the muscles in his brown throat working hard as his fingers tightened around her own.

'You say he?'

'Do you want to know the sex, Cesare?'

There was a pause before Cesare responded. 'I do not care about the sex so long as he, she, is strong and healthy.'

'Well, the way he she is moving around there seems very little problem there.' She glanced towards the doctor to seek confirmation and he nodded.

'I'm happy to say everything is as it should be.'

'In a few weeks you'll be able to feel him move, kick… I just need to make some measurements to confirm your dates.'

'Oh, there is no mistake about those,' she said without thinking.

'Indeed, a night to remember,' Cesare agreed blandly.

'I'm not blushing,' Sam lied, not looking at the doctor.

'You are,' Cesare replied, a smile in his voice.

She blushed again when the medic confirmed that her dates were spot on before wiping the gel off her stomach and leaving them alone.

'Thank you for that.'

Sam finished readjusting her clothes and got to her feet. 'For what?' Sam asked, avoiding those dark eyes and wishing she could avoid the intensity of her own feelings as easily.

'Thank you for letting me see our child through your eyes, Samantha.'

A warm glow spread through Sam as she savoured the intimacy of the moment. Her throat clogged with emotion as she replied, 'You're welcome. He is, after all, the one thing we have in common. We should be able to share that much at least.'

He appeared about to speak but then stopped and instead reached out and took her chin between his fingers. His ability to be able to place her in a room always astonished Sam. 'So you will let me see our baby through your beautiful blue eyes.'

'They are blue,' she admitted.

'Tim got quite lyrical when he described the colour to me—like violets, he tells me. This is the point where you remind me you have freckles.'

'And what do you do?'

'I kiss you,' he said, and did.

Eight days after the scan the day of the wedding dawned—no point in hanging around, Cesare had said—and Sam had been suffering panic attacks on a daily basis. It was as if the thing had gathered momentum like a snowball and run away from her.

She could have stopped the snowball effect with one word but she hadn't—because the alternative would mean a lot of things, including spending her nights alone.

They'd spent every night together except the two that Cesare had stayed over in Rome for business, and the previous night when Sam had returned to her bedsit for the last time. During the nights of passion she had no doubts; it was when daylight dawned that she started wondering about her sanity.

Maybe morning had a similar effect on Cesare, maybe he woke up wondering what he was doing? After earlier that day it seemed a distinct possibility. Why else did a man ring the woman he was marrying ten hours later that day at five-thirty in the morning?

He had rung off after ten minutes and the why was no clearer. But she had been left with the nagging impression that he had wanted to say something—possibly to call the whole thing off—and had changed his mind.

She had picked up the phone to ring him back several times but had lacked the guts to follow through.

She was still wondering about what he had intended to say when the car arrived to take her to the register office.

'It's not too late,' she told her pale reflection. But it was and she knew she was committed. This was the best thing for the baby. The best thing for her wasn't going to happen—it couldn't. Cesare didn't love her.

The discovery that she loved him had not come to her in a blinding flash.

She wasn't even sure at what point during the last week she had actually realised the truth.

When he had slid the big sapphire on her finger and she had had to turn away to hide the rush of hot emotional tears?

When she had come across the snapshot of him clinging to a vertical rock wall above a dizzying drop and realised that it was only one of the things that had been snatched from him? That he faced every day with a bravery and lack of self-pity that filled her with admiration?

She thought of the day she had walked into a room an hour before he was flying off to Rome and he had been sitting at a desk staring into space, looking so remote as he'd turned his head in her direction that a shiver of apprehension had chased its way down her spine.

What did you expect? the voice in her head had asked. *The man doesn't love you, he isn't going to tell you he's counting the minutes until he sees you again. He isn't going to say he will feel lonely when you're not there...* But she would. Had it been then that she'd realised her love for him?

It was all of those times and none of them because she knew that deep down it was something she had always known but had denied to herself. She was in love. Cesare Brunelli, brave, stubborn, and totally impossible, was the love of her life.

Today should have been the happiest of her life but instead as the car arrived at her destination all she felt was a profound sadness. The sadness that hung about her like a dark cloud had nothing to do with the fact there were no guests—it had been Sam's decision not to tell her family or friends.

Her misery arose, not from the absence of guests or an elaborate wedding, but because of the absence of the one thing her heart craved— to have her love returned. But it just wasn't going to happen.

Cesare didn't love her. He would care for her and he would, she believed, respect the vows he made because she had learnt that, unlike the person portrayed in the tabloids, he was actually a deeply honourable man. But she would never have that place in his heart she so longed for.

Was she greedy, Sam wondered, to want it so badly when she had so much?

And what would happen if one day he met someone he did love the way he had loved Candice? Did he still love the beautiful blonde? Sam couldn't stop torturing herself with the thoughts that he might have been thinking of the other woman when they made love.

The thoughts, when they intruded, made her feel sick to her stomach and they had spoilt more than one perfect moment for her, and Cesare, with his uncanny perception, always seemed to pick up on her unease.

When he asked her what was wrong, she never told him, of course. She said nothing, but he knew she was lying and the lie lay like a wall between them. It dissolved when their passions flared and ignited, but later when they cooled it was still there.

Sam knew that if this marriage was going to stand any chance of working she had to overcome her insecurities and accept that Cesare could not give her what she wanted—what he did give her was more than most women ever had.

She would make it work, she said to herself as she lifted her skirts and left the car.

Tim, looking nervous as though he were the groom, was waiting for her in the foyer of the old town hall building.

'You look beautiful,' he gasped, his eyes widening in shock when he saw Sam.

Sam touched the white skirt of her oyster satin gown with a self-conscious hand. 'You don't think it's a bit over the top?'

Sam's original intention had been to wear the suit she had worn for her brother's wedding. It had after all cost a small fortune and only been worn once.

It was not a suggestion that had found favour with Cesare, who, ignoring her protest that she hated posh shops, had rung ahead to some exclusive store and arranged for it to open out of hours for her to choose something suitably fitting for the bride of a billionaire.

She had not entered the place with any intention of purchasing anything approaching a traditional wedding gown. A suit or something simple had been her vague instruction to the helpful assistant—people became very helpful when unlimited funds were involved, Sam had realised cynically.

Maybe she hadn't been very specific because the first thing they had produced had been a dress, the one she was now wearing.

It was the simplicity that had immediately attracted her. Cut in simple strapless sheath design, the shimmering fabric kicked out slightly at the calf-length hem, but hugged her waist and hips.

She had been a little unsure about baring her shoulders and revealing so much cleavage—the boned bodice had an uplifting quality, but the staff had reassured her it was perfect.

Of course, the way they had raved might have had something to do with the cost—this was not the sort of store that had anything as tasteless as price tags—but, seeing her reflection in the mirror-lined cubicle, Sam had had to admit she didn't look too bad.

Once she had said yes to the dress the entire

thing had snowballed into some sort of mad retail-therapy frenzy! An hour later a stunned Sam had ended up being escorted back to the chauffeur-driven limo the proud owner of some sinfully sexy decadent underclothes, shoes, and most extravagantly a simply gorgeous antique Brussels lace veil.

'This is a wedding—you can't be too over the top,' Tim said as he watched the sparkle fade from her violet eyes. She looked so sad that, even though he wasn't a man into tactile displays, he wanted to hug her.

'It's not that sort of wedding.' Sam bit her lip as she heard her carefully neutral tone ruined by the emotional vibrato quiver in her response.

Tim's eyes fell from her direct gaze, but he did not directly respond to her comment or, to her relief, lie. Instead he surprised her by producing a posy from behind his back like a conjuror.

'I hope you don't mind? It *is* a wedding and you should have flowers.' Tim pressed the posy of violets into Sam's hands, adding gruffly. 'The colour reminded me of your eyes.'

Sam was incredibly touched by the unexpected

gesture. She lifted the posy to her face and inhaled. 'Thank you, you're very kind.'

'You can't have a wedding without flowers. I know—I offered to pay for the flowers for my sister's wedding.' He let out a silent whistle. 'I had no idea at the time how much they could cost in a real wedding.' He stopped and looked embarrassed. 'Not that this isn't a real wedding,' he added hastily.

'There's no need to pretend—we both know that it isn't,' Sam replied, her outward composure a stark contrast to the misery churning in her stomach.

Tim's expression grew earnest as he studied her pale face. 'Are you sure about this, Sam?'

Sam, who wasn't sure about anything except the fact Cesare was the love of her life and the father of her child, managed a teasing smile. 'Are you suggesting I run?'

'If Cesare wants this I doubt you could run fast or far enough to escape him…' Tim's eyes widened with dismay. 'God, I make him sound sinister. I didn't mean it that way, I just meant…'

That he wants this baby at any cost and I come as part of the package.

Sam sighed. She supposed she ought to be grateful that Cesare had not tried to deceive her. He had not pretended to love her. Recognising that part of her wished he *had* filled Sam with self-disgust.

'I know what you meant, Tim, he's…implacable. Don't worry, I know what I'm doing…'

Tim didn't look as though he believed that claim any more than she did.

'And if I don't, well, there is a perfectly easy solution,' she mused, recalling Cesare's comments on the subject.

'Divorce?'

Sam could understand Tim's shocked expression. After all, it wasn't customary for a bride to be discussing the subject just before she took her vows.

Her slender shoulder lifted. 'Well…it happens. Don't worry, I'll try and make it work,' she added.

It occurred to Cesare as he stood in the small anonymous room that this was not the sort of wedding that most girls dreamed of.

What sort of wedding had Samantha dreamed about?

Had she dreamed?

He didn't know because he hadn't asked her, he hadn't given her time to think. It had been obvious that she was still in a state of shock over the unplanned pregnancy and he had ruthlessly exploited the situation to coerce her into marriage. What she wanted or needed had not come into the equation. He had been totally focused on being there for his child, on being a full-time father. That focus had allowed him to ignore one simple fact—he needed her.

Cesare had never needed a woman before. Wanted, yes, but needed, no.

The fact she was carrying his child had been convenient in that it had offered a sufficient excuse for him to legitimately avoid delving too deep into the survival-instinct mentality that had taken over when he had thought of her slipping out of his life.

A wave of self-disgust rolled over him.

He was a selfish bastard, but the recognition did not lessen his determination that this ceremony would go ahead.

He would be a considerate husband, he silently vowed.

She would not regret marrying him.

The door opened with a silent swish; there was no accompanying blast of music. No tissues were lifted to blot emotional tears, no heads turned to gasp at the bride.

It took every last ounce of Cesare's self-control not to turn his own head in response to the sound of footsteps on the wood-block floor.

Sam recited her part in the charade in a quiet voice that the registrar visibly struggled to hear. Cesare in contrast made his responses in a clear, resonant tone. She kept her eyes carefully trained on the registrar throughout the service and it wasn't until Cesare was given the smiling all-clear to kiss his bride that she turned and tilted her head, her shaking fingers struggling to lift her veil.

Cesare released a sigh, glad now more than ever that he had ignored the doctor's earnest advice that morning.

Who would want to be lying in a hospital bed gazing at the sterile white walls when they could be looking at this face? She was beautiful.

He gazed, inscribing to memory every detail of her heart-shaped face. He had traced each contour with his fingers; he knew her skin was smooth and soft; he knew all about the tiny suggestion of a cleft in her small, determined chin and faint frown line between her feathery brows. He knew her mouth was lush and wide and made for kissing.

What he *didn't* know about until now was that her lips were pink like roses, the colour only enhanced, not disguised, by the clear gloss she had applied to them.

That there was the creamy glowing tint to her skin, the delicious sprinkling of freckles across the bridge of her tip-tilted nose, the glorious Titian of her Pre-Raphaelite curls, and most of all he hadn't known about the colour of her eyes, an impossible shade of deep velvet blue.

His throat tightened as emotions swelled in his chest. If he woke up tomorrow back in a world of blackness he would carry this memory, that colour, her face with him.

There had been occasions over the past days when he had fallen asleep with her in his arms fantasising about waking up in the morning and seeing her face. He had never actually expected it to happen, but it had and she had not been there.

Not there, but his first instinct had been to tell her. He had picked up the phone, his intention to do just that, to share the miracle.

Then he had heard her sleepy voice the other end and thought, *What if it isn't a miracle?* Maybe his sight would vanish as abruptly as it had returned. So he had remained silent and taken the decision instead to seek medical advice.

CHAPTER NINE

'YES, your vision has returned, Mr Brunelli.'

Cesare had struggled to stifle his impatience with the doctor. 'I did not need you to tell me that. What I need you to tell me is will it last?' Or would he wake up tomorrow in the world of blackness once more?

The medic was unwilling to commit himself. 'We have no idea if this is permanent until we do more tests, Mr Brunelli.'

'If that is so, Doctor, there are things other than your face that I would prefer to spend what time I have looking at.'

His retort drew a thin smile from the doctor, though the other man clearly didn't take his objection seriously. 'I understand, but I must recommend in the strongest terms that you remain in hospital until we have completed more tests.'

Cesare retorted in equally strong terms and in considerably more robust language that he was getting married that afternoon and nothing would keep him from that appointment.

Now, as the ceremony neared the end, he did not regret his decision. He had seen Sam's face. No one could rob him of that.

The expectation among the small wedding party stretched as Cesare froze, an odd dazed expression on his face. As if, Sam thought miserably, he had just realised the enormity of what he had done and was already regretting it.

She was seized by the humiliating certainty that he wasn't going to take up the registrar's invitation to kiss her. She was lowering her head when he reached out and cupped her chin in one hand.

'You don't have to,' she whispered as he dipped his head. Suddenly she couldn't stand the pretence, the sham. She wanted with all her heart for it to be real, but she knew it never would be. 'There is no one to act for,' she added, making her voice cold. The quiver was an addition she had no control over.

Even though she knew it wasn't possible his

eyes seemed to hold hers as his mouth feathered across her lips, soft as a butterfly caress.

'I'm not acting. We're married, *cara*,' he said, running the tip of his thumb along the outline of her lips. 'This is for real, not an act.' The throaty murmur was pitched for her ears only.

The light in his eyes dazzled her, awakening the gnawing need and longing that was always just below the surface when she was anywhere near him.

'And I kiss you because I want to and you want me to, not to satisfy an audience. You do want me to, don't you, *cara*?'

Sam had forgotten they had an audience; she was utterly mesmerised as she whispered, 'Yes.'

He brushed his lips across hers and Sam's eyes drifted shut as her lips parted under the light pressure and her fingers tightened around her posy of flowers.

The lingering kiss was so exquisitely tender that it brought a rush of hot tears to Sam's eyes. When he lifted his head she remained still, her lashes lying dark against her delicately flushed cheeks.

Cesare looked down at her face and felt a swell

of emotions so powerful that for a moment he could hardly breathe. From the instant he'd learnt about the pregnancy he'd been telling himself he was a great guy willing to make the supreme sacrifice and marry the mother of his child.

Sacrifice nothing! He'd been acting selfishly. His life would have no meaning without this in-furiating, gorgeous redhead!

She opened her eyes and they shone deep violet as she looked up at him. He felt as if someone had reached into his chest and grabbed his heart. When he told her he had got her the sack she was going to hate him.

The registrar cleared her throat and gave an apologetic smile.

'I'm sorry, but I have another couple booked in for four-thirty…'

Sam blushed and said, 'Of course…sorry…' She placed a hand unobtrusively under Cesare's elbow and murmured softly that there were two steps.

'As much as I appreciate you being sensitive to my feelings, Samantha, I think it would be a lot easier if I just lean on you.'

Sam flashed an uncertain look at his face as he pulled her into his side. 'Yes, I suppose it would.' Not easier for her, though, to maintain an illusion of cool when she was overwhelmingly conscious of the lean, hard body pressed against her own.

But that was all right because brides were not meant to be cool, they were meant to be glowing. She wasn't, but Sally, Tim's girlfriend, didn't seem to recognise there was anything lacking at least.

She was misty eyed as she kissed Sam; Cesare she regarded with nervous awe.

'Where are you going on your honeymoon?' she asked Sam as they left the building heading for the waiting limo.

'Oh, we're not having a honeymoon.'

Sally's face fell. 'Oh, what a pity!' she exclaimed.

Sam's eyes slid briefly to the tall man at her side…she'd have to get used to calling and even thinking about him as her husband. 'Cesare's got to attend a business meeting early tomorrow and—'

'We are having a honeymoon.'

Sam's jaw dropped as she tilted her face up to his. 'What?'

'A honeymoon. We are having one—didn't I say?'

'I don't understand,' Sam said when they were alone in the car. 'It was agreed we weren't having a honeymoon.' Honeymoons were meant for people in love. 'You have urgent—'

'There has been a change of plan,' Cesare inserted smoothly.

Sam's eyes narrowed. 'A plan on which I wasn't consulted!' she responded, not really understanding why she felt so cranky except that he had taken her by surprise. 'I suppose this is how it's going to be married to you. I'm supposed to fall obediently in line with anything you say because I'm a dutiful wife.'

'Anyone would think you're regretting it already.'

Sam was glad the dark eyes scanning her face could not see the tear stains. 'Is that transference?'

'Oh, my God, this is worse than I thought. You've taken psychology classes.'

'This isn't a honeymoon, is it? You're taking me with you on a damned business trip so that you can keep an eye on me…you don't trust me!' she accused shrilly.

'This is a romantic gesture, *cara*. I'm being spontaneous.'

His sarcasm seemed unnecessarily cruel to Sam, who turned her head away, an unnecessary protective gesture to hide the new tears that sprang to her eyes.

They travelled on in silence until she had governed her unpredictable emotions enough to speak without shouting or crying or both. 'Where are we going?'

'I thought it would be appropriate if we went back to where we met.'

Her jaw dropped. 'Scotland, the castle! You're joking.'

'I thought you might be pleased.'

'But my brother…'

'I did not invite him,' Cesare inserted apologetically.

She threw him a withering look and narrowed her eyes. 'Very funny, but what's he going to say when he finds out we're married?'

'I expect he will tell you that you could have done better for yourself, which you probably could, but I think if you do not mind we will delay any family reunions. There is no need for us to see anyone. I have arranged for all the necessary provisions to be delivered and have requested no housekeeping. Of course it is possible that my request will be ignored by interfering domestic help…'

Against her will Sam responded to his teasing lopsided smile.

'That's better,' he approved, leaning back in his seat.

'What's better?'

'I prefer it when you're smiling at me to when you're scowling.'

Her brow furrowed. 'How did you know I was smiling?'

'I can hear it in your voice, *cara*.'

Sam, who hoped that was all he could hear, relaxed back into the seat beside him. The only thing that made her situation bearable was the fact that Cesare didn't begin to suspect her true feelings. Her expression grew pensive as she acknowledged why it was important to her for him not to know. With little else left, pride took on an extra importance.

'Come here!' Cesare said, suddenly reaching out and drawing her to him.

Nestling into his side, Sam closed her eyes and felt some of the tension that tied her muscles in knots slip away.

'Are you pleased about the honeymoon?' Cesare asked, stroking a tendril of hair back from her smooth brow.

'I'm surprised.'

Her cautious response drew an ironic smile from him.

Aware that they had driven past the road that led to Cesare's London Georgian town house, Sam straightened up. 'Why are we going this way?'

'The helipad at the house is undergoing repairs. We're leaving from just south of—'

'We're flying to Scotland by helicopter?'

His expression suggested he was amazed she had thought otherwise.

'But I can't go like this! I haven't pack-ed and—'

Cesare disposed of her protests with a shrug and a matter-of-fact explanation. 'I'm sure you look charming like that and, as the store had your measurements, it was simple to arrange for them to send over some clothes this morning and the necessary personal items. If there's anything I have forgotten we can send down for it.'

'You've bought me an entire wardrobe?'

He raised a brow and looked amused. 'Is that a problem?'

Sam, who was sure it ought to be on principle, scowled.

'A husband is allowed to buy his wife a few clothes.'

Sam gulped and voiced her doubts out loud. 'Husband? I wonder if that will ever *not* sound strange.'

'The unfamiliar can quickly become commonplace if you allow it.'

The comment drew a laugh from Sam.

He inclined his head in an attitude of enquiry. 'That is funny?'

Sam extended a hand to touch his lean cheek and, biting her lip, drew back at the last moment.

'The idea of there being anything commonplace about you,' she confided huskily, 'is not funny, it's frankly hilarious.'

The silence between them stretched as Cesare appeared to study her face, something that Sam always found intensely unnerving.

'I think, Samantha, that might have been a compliment…?'

'It was,' she admitted, then in an effort to defuse the tension that had sprung up between them she added lightly, 'But don't let it go to your head.'

She shuffled along the seat and leaned back into the soft leather.

Cesare made no comment on the space she had put between them, but he did suggest she could take a nap on the flight up to Scotland.

Sam, who was no longer amazed by his spooky perception lifted a hand to stifle a yawn. The effects of the last twenty-four hours were catching up on her, but she expressed her doubt that she'd be able to sleep during the flight.

She was wrong.

She closed her eyes just to rest them shortly after they took off and the next thing she knew Cesare was shaking her awake.

'We're here already?'

'Time passes swiftly when one is snoring.'

'I didn't!' she protested.

'No,' he conceded, 'you just gently slobbered all over my shoulder.'

His eyes were so warm as they rested on her face that, despite the fact he wasn't really seeing her, Sam subsided in blushing confusion. He, of course, looked predictably gorgeous, and Sam took the opportunity to stare. While she had to be guarded in her speech, at least she did not have to disguise her feelings behind clever banter or hostility when she looked at him. A sigh left her lips as her hungry gaze sank to his wide, sensual mouth.

Paolo, who had been travelling up front with the pilot, carried their luggage into the castle and spoke briefly to Cesare before vanishing into the gathering darkness.

Moments later Sam heard the chopper taking off.

She turned to look at Cesare and as their eyes connected she had to tell herself for the umpteenth time that day that he couldn't actually see her, he just had very expressive eyes. Unable to look away, she was suddenly overwhelmed by shyness.

'Which is ridiculous.'

Cesare lowered his gaze, tugged his tie off and asked, 'What is ridiculous?'

'Feeling like a virgin on my wedding night is ridiculous…because I'm not…obviously.' Her hand went to her stomach.

Something flashed in his eyes, a strong emotion but one that Sam couldn't define. 'Do you regret it?'

She shook her head, confused by the harshness of his abrupt question.

'Do you regret sleeping with me that night?'

Sam shook her head again from side to side. 'No,' she admitted huskily. 'I don't.'

Sam felt a flutter of panic in the pit of her stomach. This was the closest she had ever come to admitting the extent of her feelings for Cesare.

She closed her eyes and silently willed him not to press her further on the subject. If he did she didn't know what she'd say. Sometimes just lately she was as surprised as him to hear the things that came out of her mouth.

When he didn't respond she opened her eyes, instantly colliding with his dark stare. There had never been anything empty about Cesare's sightless eyes. They were an accurate reflection of his emotions, and intelligence always shone in those obsidian depths.

She experienced a flash of reckless bravery and challenged, 'Do you regret anything?'

If he were was a better man, Cesare reflected, he would.

'I regret…' he began slowly.

Sam's fingers clenched into tight fists at her sides. She lifted her chin and forced a breath past the lump of despair in her throat.

Was she some sort of masochist? Why had she asked him? Why did she invite this?

And why wouldn't he regret it? The one night of sex had cost him dear. Sleeping with her had thrown his life into total chaos—it had obliged him to give up his freedom and marry a woman that he barely knew.

'Fine, I understand.' Without looking at him she picked up a kettle, filled it from the tap and placed it with an unsteady hand on the hob.

'I regret, Samantha, that your introduction to lovemaking was not…gentler and more considerate.'

It was as much the self-recrimination in his voice as the stilted delivery of his words that made her spin back in startled amazement.

'I wouldn't change it—any of it!' she said fiercely.

'And I regret that I contrived to have you sacked.'

Her lips quivered as she tried to smile, though it was not her idea of a joke and he was not smiling. 'Very funny, but I think you overrate your influence, Cesare.'

'Did losing your job not influence your decision when I proposed we get married?'

Her nose wrinkled as she recalled the frightful day. 'I suppose it did,' she admitted, still not seeing where this was going.

'It was meant to and I do have that much influence. It took one phone call…' Cesare knew he was taking a risk but it was best she heard it from him rather than finding out some other way some time down the line.

With the vows they had made still fresh in his

mind he didn't want to start married life with this deceit on his conscience.

'You did that?'

He nodded.

'Why?'

The bewildered hurt in her voice made him flinch. 'My father was not around when I was growing up. I do not want that for my child. I would have moved mountains to bring about our marriage, Samantha. I didn't want to leave anything to chance.'

'And never mind whose dreams you trample over?' A slightly hysterical laugh was drawn from her lips. 'At least I know I wasn't such a lousy writer.'

'Sam…'

She lifted a hand and shook her head. 'Not now, Cesare.'

'Samantha!'

She heard her name, but didn't stop as she fled the room. Then she broke down and wept, tears running unchecked down her face.

She had walked through several rooms of the castle before she registered the huge bowls of sweet-smelling flowers that permeated each room with their scent, a scent that was intensified by the warmth from the open fires that appeared to have been lit in the stone hearths of all the rooms.

She thought about her sister-in-law going from room to room to inspect the preparations for their important guests and she shook her head. It made her smile to imagine their amazement when they discovered that *she* was one of those guests. Though it would be nothing to their amazement when they discovered she was married!

She bent over one of the vases and inhaled the heady fragrance, then heaved a deep sigh before straightening her shoulders. Her emotions had never felt this close to the surface.

When she re-entered the kitchen Cesare was standing in the exact spot he had been when she ran out. His expression was inscrutable but the air around him vibrated with tension.

Sam said the first thing that came into her head. 'Would you like a cup of tea?'

His lips twitched, but to her relief some of

the tension in the air receded, making it easier to breathe.

He leaned back against the counter and stood there, his arms folded across his chest. 'Why not?' He gave a shrug and added quietly, 'I am not proud of what I did, you know.'

'I wonder if there's milk?' Then she stopped, bit her lip and fixed him with a wide candid stare. 'It was a vile thing to do, but I suppose you didn't have to tell me and that at least is something.'

Cesare stopped himself asking if it was enough as he watched Sam open the fridge.

Her eyes opened wide as she saw the contents. There wasn't just milk and basics, it was an Aladdin's cave. There was just about every luxury item of food you could imagine plus several bottles of champagne. She lifted one out, looked at the label and whistled before putting it back and taking out a carton of milk.

'It's a pity I'm not allowed alcohol.'

'I will keep you company with the orange juice.'

Sam closed the door. 'You don't have to,' she said, wishing she didn't have to love him so utterly and totally. 'Why did you tell me?'

'I didn't want to start this marriage with a lie, but I forgot that the truth, *cara*, is not always better.' In fact the truth could be highly overrated.

'Of course the truth is better!' she exclaimed.

'The truth, Samantha, is that you married me because you were desperate and I was your meal ticket.'

The pragmatic description caused the hot colour to rush to her cheeks. 'You think that?' How could a man as bright as him not know she loved him?

His dark brows lifted. 'I'm hardly in a position to criticise, Samantha.'

No, but he did just think she was a variation on an avaricious gold-digger. She heaved a silent sigh. Maybe that was actually better than him knowing the truth. 'You think I married you for your money?'

And wasn't he right?

But nothing as Sam knew to her cost, was as simple as it looked.

Since the moment when she had seen the look upon Cesare's face as she had described their unborn child to him it had been an uphill struggle to continue to think of Cesare as the two-dimensional, cold, ruthless despot with a chip on his shoulder she had origninally labelled him.

He was a far more complex man, a fascinating man of strong passions whose worst sins were not loving her and his willingness to do anything for his unborn child.

'I think you saddled yourself with a blind husband because you want the best for your child. You're the last woman in the world I'd accuse of being avaricious, Samantha.'

'You could have told me before the wedding,' she pointed out.

'I'm not that much of a reformed character, Samantha.'

'Are your parents together?'

He shook his head. 'My father walked out when I was ten, my mother remarried a few years later and I moved out when I was sixteen. Family is something I never had.'

Sam could read the hurt and loneliness behind the bald facts he outlined and, while she didn't forgive what he had done, she could understand what had driven him to do it. His determination to get married made even more sense now, but the fact that this marriage had always been about the baby made her sad and happy at the same time.

In a perfect world, even in this world for some lucky ones, a loving husband and a father willing to do anything for his child would not be mutually exclusive.

But in her world it was, so she'd better get used to it. She could have him but not his heart. She closed her eyes, not wanting to even think about what it would feel like if he gave that heart to another woman one day.

That was her nightmare.

'Well, you have one now, so don't blow it,' she advised him. 'And remember you're on probation so any time you feel any Machiavellian impulses take a shower.'

'I don't deserve you,' he said with more humility than she ever imagined to see him display.

'Hold that thought,' she said, putting the milk back into the fridge.

'We will celebrate together with champagne after the baby is born.'

She turned her head and was startled to find he

was standing at her elbow, close enough for her to smell the clean male scent of his body. A stab of sexual longing knifed through her body, snatching the breath from her lungs with its intensity.

'It is a big thing you have done, Samantha.'

'Well, I want this marriage to work too. I had the things you missed out on, Cesare. I had a great childhood and I'd like that for my baby.' She sucked in a deep breath and pushed her hair back from her face.

'I could make something to eat if you like— steak and salad…?' Without waiting for his response she added quickly, 'I don't know about you but I'm starving so I'll just go change out of these things.' She flashed a quick smile in his general direction and left the room.

Outside the room she leaned against the door…and closed her eyes. So far she was handling herself with all the skill of a dancer with two left feet—and both of those seemed to be permanently in her mouth. She had been within a heartbeat of blurting out that the only reason she had forgiven him was because she loved him!

Upstairs in the largest of the bedrooms she

found the clothes that Cesare had promised laid out in neat piles on the big four-poster bed.

What she needed, she told herself, was a coping strategy.

But what?

With a sigh she stepped out of her dress and, after folding it carefully and placing it on the bed, walked to the big mullioned window that gave a view of the loch.

She had absolutely no idea how long she stood there lost in thought. It was only when she began to shiver with cold—the basque she wore was not really intended for wearing in the Scottish Highlands—that she realised the moon was out and shining its silvery light over the surface of the water far below. With a sigh she began to pull the heavy brocade curtains across the window.

'Leave that.'

Sam, who hadn't heard him come into the room, started at the sound of Cesare's voice. She turned and saw his tall figure framed in the doorway, a towel knotted around his middle and his jet hair dripping wet.

Her breath quickened as her covetous gaze slid

over the perfect definition of his broad chest before sliding lower to his flat belly. She ran her tongue across her dry lips as her heart rate quickened.

'I thought you were downstairs.' She was startled to realise she had been gone long enough for him to shower.

His shoulders lifted. 'As you see, I am not.'

'You should have called me.' She was angry because in her head she could see him lying unconscious at the bottom of the stairs that were uneven stone and lethally steep. The castle did not boast anything as modern as en suite facilities and the nearest bathroom was up a winding staircase. 'How did you…?'

'It is always easier to get my bearings when I have been some place before,' he reminded her slickly. 'I managed on my own.'

'So I see.' She was seeing a lot more, and trying very hard not to! The towel was very small and his body was nothing short of perfect.

The way she was staring at him sent flames of lust through Cesare's body. He was seeing Samantha with her feelings bare on her face. Having her look as though the sight of him was enough to make her weak with lust was intoxicating and more of a turn-on than anything in his life.

If he told her he could see she would retreat.

There was no hurry to tell her and tomorrow there might be no need. The knowledge that this might be transitory and that he would be a fool not to enjoy it while he could swung his brief internal debate in the direction of subterfuge.

'There are some things, however, that I would prefer not to do alone.'

The suggestive warmth in his voice deepened the flush in her cheeks.

'There is being independent,' she murmured, finding it hard to speak because he looked so rampantly male and unbelievably sexy. She would have found it even harder had he known she was standing there wearing the provocative lacy basque, heels and not a lot else but goose bumps!

'And then there is plain stupidity.'

She reached again for the curtains.

'Don't.'

'Don't what?'

'Don't close the curtains. Let the moonlight in.'

He intercepted her quizzical look and added

lightly, 'No one can see in.' *And I want to see the moonlight on your body when I make love to you*, he added silently.

CHAPTER TEN

SAM frowned. 'How do you know there's a moon…?'

'These things follow a fairly predictable pattern and you said it was a clear night.'

'I did?'

'Earlier.'

Sam shrugged and stepped back.

Cesare walked past her towards the window, his confident tread slowing a little as he approached the opposite end of the room. It was almost as though sometimes he'd forgotten he was blind.

A wave of intense sadness washed over her. No doubt he wished he could forget. Maybe he did in his dreams. Maybe there were mornings when he opened his eyes and reached for the light only to realise a moment later that there was no light and never would be.

Sam watched as he turned, and her breath caught sharply. Standing there he was a magnificent commanding figure, rampantly male, a god of legend brought to life by the silvered light from the moon, which cast a glistening glow over his bronzed skin.

'Did you marry me despite the fact I am blind or because of it?'

Sam sat on the bed, drew her knees up to her chest and rested her chin on the plateau. 'What sort of question is that?'

'A woman married to a blind man could hide many things from him…'

'I haven't got anything to hide from you.'

'What are you wearing?'

Sam glanced down and gulped. 'Nothing.'

His gleaming eyes narrowed. 'Excellent.'

'I mean nothing special,' she said, a hint of desperation creeping into her voice.

'Describe it,' he commanded.

Describe it! Sam went hot and cold, then hot all over again at the thought of describing the seductive items she was almost wearing.

'Be my eyes like you were when you shared the images in the scan with me.'

Better not to be wearing anything at all, Sam decided, struggling frantically to unfasten the multiple eyelet fasteners that held the edges of the garment together. As she dealt with the last one she rose to her feet, stepped out of her shoes and peeled off the stockings. Then she allowed the gaping basque to slide to the floor with a soft silken rush.

The breath froze in Cesare's chest as desire roared like a furnace in his blood. Sam stood in the moonlight, a pale figure with softly rounded hips, slim legs and small, totally perfect breasts.

She planted her hands on her narrow hips and lifted her chin. 'I was wearing white cotton but I've taken them off.' It was only half a lie.

Cesare didn't reply, he just carried on staring. His heavy-lidded eyes seemed trained directly on her body, and Sam could hear the audible sound of his shallow respirations across the room. Even though she knew he couldn't see her she suddenly felt intensely conscious of her naked state. Now stripping off seemed less of the good idea it had done moments before.

She had on occasions wondered if her extraordinary lack of inhibitions with him was to do with the fact he couldn't see her, but she had decided on reflection that she was able to enjoy her own body for the simple reason that Cesare so obviously took pleasure from it too.

She ran her tongue across the outline of her dry lips. 'Do you think there's another storm coming? I can feel something in the air.'

'It's called sexual tension, *cara*,' he slurred. 'And a person is meant to feel it on her wedding night.'

'Be careful,' she cried as he began to cross the room towards her with a panther-like speed. 'You'll…' The words clogged in her throat as he pulled her into his arms.

Fortune was obviously on his side as by some freak of luck he'd reached her without touching one of the several obstacles that had stood in the way of his impetuous progress.

'I'll what?' he asked, drawing a line with his finger down her cheek and breathing, '*Dio mio*, but you're so beautiful.'

'You'll hurt yourself,' she whispered. Even squeezing her eyes tightly shut did not block out the sybaritic image of him that was printed on her retina.

'Nothing could hurt me as much as not being inside you very soon.'

She lifted her chin and looked at him through the screen of her dark lashes. 'Very soon would be good for me,' she admitted.

With an exultant cry low in his throat Cesare lifted his bride onto their marriage bed and, tossing aside the towel that covered his hips, joined her.

When the light came Cesare lay looking at Sam's sleeping face. Head turned to one side, her cheeks were flushed and her small breasts rose and fell in tune with the soft sound of her respirations.

He should have told her, he thought. There had been several occasions during the night when the confession had been on the tip of his tongue, but he had held back, not wanting to spoil the moment. Because one thing he was totally sure of was that when she did find out Samantha was going to be mad as hell.

It was close to eight and she still showed no

sign of waking when he decided to go downstairs and satisfy his hunger pangs.

Once downstairs the charm of the fresh Highland morning, rare in its crystal clarity, lured him outdoors. The peace of his surroundings calmed Cesare's restless mood as his route led him over heather that was springy underfoot and still drenched with dew. The stunning backdrop of the craggy purple-topped mountain range was mirrored faithfully in the still, deep loch water. Responding to the sort of impulse that over the past months he had been forced to subdue, Cesare whipped off his white tee shirt and, wearing only his shorts, stepped into the icy water.

He waded to waist depth and dived smoothly beneath the sparkling surface, swimming with no particular purpose, just enjoying the sensation of being this close to the elements. He didn't stop until he was several hundred metres from the shore, when he flipped lazily onto his back and lay there floating until his heart rate slowed. It was only when he began to tread water in anticipation of swimming back that he became aware of the hoarse cries emanating from the shoreline.

Without wasting time on pointless speculation, he began to swim back to the shore and the shrill shouts. Then he saw that Samantha was floundering out of her depth. *'Madre di Dio*, what are you doing?'

Sam took one look into his face and stopped fighting. She wept softly as he towed her back to dry land.

Her arms were still curled around his neck as he carried her out of the water and she was shaking hard. He set her on her feet and without a sound she slid down onto the heather and sat there holding her head in her hands, her shoulders heaving as she continued to silently weep.

Her misery made no impact on the rage that ripped through Cesare, who dropped on one knee beside her and demanded roughly, 'What in God's name were you doing?'

Her head lifted and her red-rimmed eyes focused on his face. 'Me?' she echoed. 'What was I doing? You could have drowned. Oh, God, I thought you had!' She squeezed her eyes tight shut, but was unable to turn off the nightmare images in her head. 'I know you don't want to make any concession to your disability, Cesare, but you're blind. I'm sorry if that hurts, but you are and you can't swim out into the middle of a loch alone that way. It was nothing short of suicidal!' she accused.

'You were trying to save me.'

The sound of his amazed laughter made Sam see red. The faint unease she had felt waking up alone had grown into full-scale mind-numbing panic by the time she'd found his tee shirt at the water's edge—and he was laughing!

'We all make mistakes.' She glared at him as she thought how she had never seen anything as beautiful as him now.

Through the skein of her wet lashes she stared, things twisting low inside her as her glance slid over his lean, muscle-ridged torso. His skin glistened with the water that streamed down his face and body, and the wet fabric of his shorts had slipped down low on his narrow hips. Drenched, they did a very poor job of concealing anything from her hungry gaze.

His eyes were drawn back to the still water and his smile faded as a shudder ran down his spine. 'What were you thinking of, jumping into the freezing water that way?'

Sam lowered her eyes and stopped wringing the water from her hair; the stern reproach in his tone made her jaw drop.

'What was *I* thinking of?'

'You're pregnant—you can't run around doing crazy things.'

Her expression froze into a stiff belligerent scowl. This was about the baby—of course it was, why did she expect otherwise? 'So I'm selfish. For sheer hypocrisy you really do take the prize, Cesare,' she remarked bitterly. 'Were you thinking about the baby and what a great father you were going to be when you decided to pull that suicidal stunt?'

His brow creased in concern as he touched a discoloured area on the side of her cheek with his thumb. 'You're going to have a bruise there,' he observed, shaking his head slowly from side to side. 'I was never in any danger, Samantha. I can see.'

She stopped dead, the colour seeping from her skin. 'See…?' Her wide eyes flew to his face.

He arched a brow and said simply, 'Yes.'

Her hand went to her mouth and her violet eyes grew saucer-round. 'You can see?'

Her initial intense joy was quickly diluted by suspicion. 'How…why…when…?'

'The first two are open to question, the last I can answer. I woke up yesterday and I could see.'

'You woke up yesterday and you could see.' Sam could do no more than echo his words in stunned disbelief as her thought processes struggled to catch up with the information.

He inclined his dark head. 'Yes…' His dark eyes slid down her slim body, the nightdress she was wearing clung to every delicious dip and curve. 'You should come indoors and get dry,' he said throatily.

Sam saw the direction of his gaze and lifted a hand to cover her breasts, a self-conscious chill crawling across her already icy skin. Even if a couple of people had not already commented on the fact Sam knew that Cesare had a type and she was not it—actually she could not be farther from it!

It wasn't that she had a problem with the way

she looked, but she knew she was nothing special and Cesare was accustomed to special.

He was special.

Although if he was struggling to hide his disappointment at her appearance he was doing it well, she conceded, unable to maintain eye contact with his bold black stare.

'You can see and you didn't think this might be something you should mention in passing?' she wondered with biting sarcasm. 'You know, something along the lines of— Oh, by the way, Sam, I can see!'

Her heaving breasts strained against their wet confinement as her indignation rose to new heights. 'When were you going to tell me, or were you going to tell me at all?'

'I have told you now, have I not?' He dismissed the subject with an autocratic wave of his hand, picked up his tee shirt from the ground and draped it over her shoulders. 'Come on, you can't stay here.'

Sam didn't move an inch. Shaking like a leaf, she just stared at him. 'My God, you are unbelievable!' she breathed. 'You can't drop something like this on me and act as if nothing has happened. I'm not going anywhere until you…' She stopped, her widened gaze flying to his face. 'You went through the wedding ceremony pretending…' She closed her eyes—*their marriage was all pretence.*

'I was not pretending. If you had asked me I would have replied honestly.'

'That's twisting the facts and you know it!' she raged while recognising in retrospect that there had been several clues during the day and last night she might have picked up on.

Though as he made few concessions to his blindness she sometimes completely forgot about it, so maybe her belated recognition was not that surprising.

Her lips suddenly quivered. 'You knew what I was wearing last night and you were laughing at me.'

Desire roared in his blood as he thought about her unhooking that sinfully provocative lace number.

'I was not laughing,' he promised.

How did she imagine any man with a red-blood corpuscle in his body could laugh or even think when she had stood there looking like the living, breathing epitome of every erotic male fantasy?

'Look, I can see, it happened, a miracle, luck, it does not matter what you call it, my sight has returned. You've got no shoes on.' The horrified discovery brought a fresh swell of concern to his chest. 'Let me carry you…'

'Go away!' she snarled, turning her back on him as she began to trace her steps up the incline towards the castle.

His eyes narrowed on her slim, rigid back. 'Anyone would think from your attitude that you would prefer my sight hadn't returned!'

The outrageous charge drew a gasp from her lips as she whirled back. 'That,' she told him in a shaking voice, 'is a totally vile thing to say! This marriage is based on a web of lies and deceit and I've had enough of it and you.'

She had only taken two steps before she was swept quite literally off her feet. She held herself rigid in his arms and fought the impulse to burrow her face into the convenient gap between his shoulder and chin.

It wasn't until he had kicked the kitchen door

shut behind them that she looked at him, and even then she didn't allow her glance to linger long at the uncompromising angle of his stubble covered jaw—he looked combustible!

'I don't know what you've got to be angry about,' she grumbled.

He lifted a brow. 'You don't?'

Sam was not fooled by his conversational tone. She could tell from the tension in every muscle of his incredible body that he was furious.

'Well, let me explain the facts of life, Samantha—based on lies or not, this marriage is here to last.'

'Where are you taking me?' she wailed as he began to take the stone staircase at a run. 'You think you can make me agree to anything if you take me to bed.'

He turned his head, smiled unpleasantly and said, 'I'm not taking you to bed.'

A wave of mortified colour spread across her skin as Sam swallowed. 'Oh.'

The bathroom door responded to another kick. 'Take that thing off,' he said, turning on the taps of the bath.

'A please would be nice,' she muttered, but did as he suggested anyway.

When he turned back she was standing there wrapped in a large fluffy bath towel.

'Get in—it will get your circulation moving.'

A glitter of challenge entered her violet eyes as they clashed with his bold dark stare. 'A little privacy would be nice.'

He looked amused. 'Nice, but it's not going to happen. Don't worry, *cara*, I've seen it all before, remember, and for the record I like it a lot.' He broke off and dragged a not quite steady hand through his dark hair before reaching out and pulling the towel from her grasp.

Her skin tingling where his smouldering gaze slid slowly down her body, Sam let out a yelp and jumped into the water, immersing herself in the concealing bubbles.

'If I wake up blind tomorrow I at least want to have seen you once.'

Sam suddenly stiffened. Her face creased into tense lines of anxiety as she pulled herself upright in the water.

'What do you mean "wake up blind"? Is that

going to happen? Cesare, tell me the truth,' she warned. 'I won't be fobbed off.'

Distracted by the water dripping off her pink-tipped quivering breasts, Cesare didn't immediately respond.

'Madre di Dio!' he breathed reverently before adding throatily, 'You're perfect, *cara.'*

Sam struggled to retain her poise—not easy when she was stark naked—as it was impossible not to be seriously aroused by the shaken sincerity in his voice and the lustful, earthy appreciation in his dark eyes.

She stood up, whipped a towel off the hamper and cloaked herself in it before stepping from the water. 'Well, you don't get to see any more until you talk.'

Cesare looked startled by her action before reluctant amusement spread across his face. 'That's blackmail…' He stopped smiling as her defiant pose slipped and he saw the real terror behind her mask of bravado and spikiness.

The fear in her eyes shook him deeply and the fact he was responsible for putting it there didn't improve matters. He was accustomed to making decisions and accepting the consequences, but he'd never previously had to consider how his choices might affect anyone else.

It was an aspect to marriage he had not considered.

'Please, Cesare….'

'Relax,' he soothed. 'Nobody said I'm going to wake up blind tomorrow.'

Nobody said… The distinction was not lost on Sam.

'That means in Cesare speak that nobody said you *wouldn't*. Surely, there are tests?' she protested. 'They can't expect you to live with the uncertainty—it's inhuman! You need to see another doctor.'

'I understand there are investigations,' he conceded reluctantly.

Sam was outraged and horrified by this evidence of gross medical incompetence. 'Then why didn't they do them?'

He sidestepped the question with a shrug and a laconic, 'What will be will be.'

His fatalistic take on the situation made Sam want to hit him.

'And I had no time for tests, I had a wedding to attend to. Nothing,' he declared, staring straight at her, 'was going to keep me away from that.'

She blinked and sniffed as her eyes filled with emotional tears of intense joy. There were two miracles! He could see, and he loved her! Sam struggled with the dangerous urge to babble back that she felt the same way, but her innate caution intervened.

'It wasn't?'

He shook his head. 'Obviously not. I want everything legal and in black and white including our marriage. That meant the lawyers could draw up the details of a trust fund for the baby. I don't think there will be anything in it you won't approve of…?'

Sam's silly smile dissolved, but thankfully she kept hold of her self-control. For someone who felt as if they had just had their hopeful heart stamped on she managed a very composed, 'I trust your judgement on anything financial.'

It was certainly better than her own judgement on anything romantic, she thought bitterly.

Maybe she hadn't managed to be as composed as she thought, because now he seemed to be looking at her oddly. The man had read her mind when he couldn't see; now she might as well give him a dated recording of her inner dialogue—that should give him a laugh or two.

She bit her lip and lowered her gaze, feeling utterly mortified and like a wishful, romantic idiot—how could she have imagined he was in love with her?

She needed to grow up! The only thing that she and Cesare had in common was this accidental baby.

The sex was good—actually incredible! But then Cesare was a highly sexed sensual male. It would have been naive to assume that love and sex were co-dependent for him.

If only she could say the same!

She had nearly made a fatal mistake when for that split second she had jumped to the assumption that it was his impatience to make her his wife that had made him behave with such reckless disregard for his health.

She wouldn't do that again.

'I told the doctor that I'll contact him when we get back to London and when I have time…'

Sam's head came up and her suspicious eyes swept his face. 'My God, they wanted you to stay in hospital and you refused! How could I have been so slow?' Sam lifted her hands to her head in an agitated motion, not registering that her towel slipped a vital inch, or that the creamy upper slopes of her breasts drew his hot gaze like a magnet.

'You are a total imbecile,' she raged, her anger intensified by the icy-cold fingers of panic that clutched at her. 'You might even have done irreparable damage.'

'Do not be so melodramatic, Samantha. As I said, I will see the doctor when we go back next week.'

'Melodramatic! Next week!' she shrilled. 'If you don't stop being so damned laid-back, I might just kill you myself!'

The threat drew a grin from him that Sam responded to with a dark frown.

'You actually think I'm going to stay here now when you should be in hospital?' A stab of paralysing fear dragged a harsh dry sob from her throat. 'You're the most selfish man I know!' she intoned, her voice shaking as her luminous eyes glared at him.

The strength of her passionate condemnation shook and baffled him.

Though things became clearer when she added, 'I wish I could forget I was about to be a parent the way you obviously can… Do you think this is the way I intended my life to be? Well, it isn't!'

His head jerked back as though she had struck him and there were dark lines etched along his cheekbones as he responded in a voice of chilling hauteur, 'You have not acted as though life with me is that distasteful.'

'You're a great lover,' she admitted, her eyes falling from his. 'And not *always* impossible,' she conceded gruffly, 'which is a plus, but we didn't get married for the sex or because we're in love or anything.' The laugh she then made was meant to show him that such a thought had never crossed her mind. Unfortunately the shrill manic bray that came out suggested it was a distinct possibility she didn't have a mind.

'Perish the thought,' he inserted sardonically.

The dry inflection brought her narrowed eyes to his face, but his expression was inscrutable as he spoke.

'We're getting married because of the baby—you know there are probably worse reasons. I know piles of people who get married for love and hate one another before the first anniversary.'

'Whereas we have a head start already—you hate me now.'

Sam frowned at the frivolous retort. 'I don't hate you, I'm just angry because you don't seem to appreciate it's a parent's duty to stay healthy for their children.'

Of course if theirs had been a conventional marriage she could have shouted about how if he cared about *her* he wouldn't take stupid risks!

But he didn't care about her—certainly not in the way her soul craved.

'This baby is why we're getting married. You seem to have forgotten that,' she reminded him again.

His perfect mouth twisted into a smile that left

his spectacular eyes as bleak as she had seen them. 'I do, don't I? Don't worry, Samantha, I understood every word of your lecture.'

'So we're leaving now?'

He laid a hand on her shoulder and without thinking Sam turned her head and rubbed her cheek against it. 'Samantha, we can't leave until this afternoon.'

She slid him a distrustful look from through her lashes. 'But you will go and let the doctors do their tests?'

'I will go,' he agreed. 'You are overreacting but I will go.'

'How can you have been so stupid?' She shook her head in weary disbelief.

'Let it go, Samantha. I think you have made your point.'

She recognised this was good advice but she couldn't follow it. 'You're an intelligent man— or at least I thought so.'

'My attitude to regaining my sight was why question a gift when you receive it—why wait to enjoy it? If losing my sight has taught me one thing, *cara*, it is never waste a single moment.

Extract the last shred of joy, enjoy what you have before fate decides to snatch it away.'

He took her by the shoulders and fitted her stiff, unyielding body into his. Pulling the towel over her shoulders and cupping the back of her head with one hand, he held her tight against him. They stood there motionless and not speaking. Cesare felt the exact moment the tension drained from her body, when her knees suddenly sagged and she went as limp as a rag doll.

With a muttered imprecation he scooped her up and carried her back to the bedroom. He pulled back the duvet and laid her down on the crisp cotton sheet before joining her.

His eyes touched the vivid skein of silky waves spread out on the pillow. 'With your hair that way you look like a little mermaid.' A sleepy mermaid who was struggling to keep her eyes open. 'You're tired.'

'I think maybe I just need to close my eyes for a bit. They say the tiredness isn't as bad in the second trimester.'

She fell asleep almost immediately and Cesare reflected that while fate had brought them together it was time that it took a back seat. He was going to take charge of the situation himself.

Sam was in the shower when the door opened. Cesare stood there looking preposterously sexy in jeans and a white open-necked shirt that emphasised the golden Mediterranean glow of his skin.

She lifted a hand to cover her breasts, which were slippery wet and coated with suds. The heat flared between her thighs as she stared at him.

'Go away! Isn't a person allowed any privacy?'

The half-hearted complaint drew a grin. 'No, but if you drop the soap I'll pick it up.'

Sam looked at the soap in her hand and sighed. She was tempted, God knew she was, but the helicopter that was to fly them back to London was due any minute and she was running late. Cesare had let her sleep and when she had woken in his arms they had made love.

Sam had lost all sense of time and the only urgency she had felt was to have Cesare inside her, and make her feel complete.

His lovemaking had been exquisitely tender and all the time he had held her gaze right up to the moment that the shattering climax had ripped through her.

'It's rude to stare.' Although she could, she knew, have been accused of the same lack of manners herself.

'I'm allowed to stare—I have a special dispensation. I was blind so I'm appreciating things I wouldn't have given a second glance before.'

Sam's body stiffened. 'Things like me, you mean?' She immediately bit her lip and reached for a towel muttering, 'Damn,' under her breath.

Cesare's brow puckered as he pushed the towel into her hands but didn't release it. 'I haven't the faintest idea why you feel so insecure, Samantha. Have I not shown you that I find you beautiful? Have I not told you?'

His fingertips brushed hers and the tingling electrical charge fizzed down to her toes. Pupils huge, she released a fractured sigh and nodded. 'Yes, you have,' she admitted. He said many things that she wanted to believe and an equal number that made her blush. Cesare was not inhibited when it came to such matters. He was very eloquent, though a lot of the Italian that he slid into in moments of passion was slightly wasted on her.

'And how often do I have to tell you before you believe me?' he asked quietly.

'I'll tell you when I know,' she said quietly.

Cesare shook his head in an attitude of baffled resignation as he relinquished his purchase on the towel. Sam immediately wrapped it sarong-wise around her body.

'Then I will just have to try harder.'

Before Sam could express her approval of this plan there was the unmistakable din of a helicopter outside the open window.

'Are you sure that you want to go back today?' she asked, before raising a brow and giving him a long meaningful look until Cesare shrugged and lifted his hands in a gesture of defeat.

He was at the door when she spoke.

'Cesare, no matter what happens with your sight…we…we'll be all right.'

CHAPTER ELEVEN

IT WAS twenty-four hours before the medical team had reviewed the results of the battery of investigations Cesare had been subjected to.

It had felt like a very long twenty-four hours to Sam—the longest in her life. As she waited for the verdict her throat felt dry and she felt physically sick with apprehension. And as they sat in the doctor's office ironically it was *Cesare* who gave *Sam's* hand a reassuring squeeze as the consultant settled in his chair.

Apparently it wasn't a miracle the doctor explained. There was a perfectly sound medical explanation of what had occurred. The doctor then went into this in some detail, even drawing a diagram that Sam struggled to display a suitable degree of interest in.

Cesare asked a couple of intelligent questions

in the appropriate places. Sam wasn't sure she could speak at all above the rising roar of panic in her ears.

She held on until the doctor started recounting a similar case a colleague of his had dealt with in the States, at which point she thought, *Enough is enough!*

She sprang to her feet without warning, causing the medical man to break off mid-anecdote and said loudly, 'Yes, that's very interesting, but what I need to know is, is he cured? Is Cesare going to be all right…permanently?'

The consultant fiddled with his half-moon glasses and looked slightly surprised. 'Let me put it this way, I wish I had your husband's vision, Mrs Brunelli.'

Sam sank to her seat as her knees gave way. She swallowed and gritted a bright, 'Good. I'm glad.'

Cesare shot her a sideways look and added, 'So am I, *cara*,' with what Sam considered super-human restraint considering the circumstances.

She took no part in the rest of the conversation and by the time they departed she had almost stopped shaking.

Neither spoke as they drove through the heavy traffic.

Cesare was infuriatingly laid-back. Then suddenly a newsreader on the radio announced that the billionaire Cesare Brunelli, who had been tragically blinded after bravely going to the aid of a child trapped in a burning car, had regained his sight.

'They said you rescued a child from a burning car?' Sam pinned her questioning gaze on Cesare's profile.

'Did they?'

'Yes, they did, you know they did! You told me that you were blind following a surgical procedure,' she reminded him.

'And so it was. I had fractured my skull and there was some inter-cranial bleeding.'

'You fractured your skull saving a child from a burning car?' He made it sound like going to the shop for a loaf of bread.

'It was barely smouldering. It didn't explode until I got her out.' That explosion had thrown him and the child he'd carried to the other side of the carriageway.

Sam wasn't fooled for a moment; she knew he was playing it down for all he was worth. Her blood froze when she thought about the danger he had undoubtedly been in. 'So actually you didn't do anything much.'

'I just happened to be there,' he agreed, looking distinctly uncomfortable. 'Anybody would have done the same.'

'I doubt that.' She planted her chin in her palm and studied his face, a smile playing around her lips. 'I really never thought I'd see you look embarrassed,' she admitted. 'That might even be a blush,' she teased, flicking his cheek.

Cesare turned his scowling face her way for an instant before focusing his attention on the road and advising her to stop talking nonsense. 'I am not a hero, I was just in the right place at the right time.'

Considering the outcome, Sam would have thought that many people would not have called it the 'right place'. 'All right, if you're more comfortable with it I'll consider you a villain. How was the little girl?'

'It was touch and go for a while,' he said.

'But she's fine now and the media stuff has died down.'

'Media stuff?'

'Yes. They love labels. I was the hero, but at the expense of the parents, who were demonized in the press. They got out of the car when Lilly was still in the back seat, but the journalists never mentioned the fact that the father had dragged the mother clear and then collapsed himself.'

Well, that explained his dislike of the press. 'That was awful,' she agreed. 'But there is such a thing as responsible reporting.'

Cesare tapped the radio and raised a significant brow. 'Like that.'

Sam accepted the point with a rueful grin of acknowledgment. 'But how on earth can they know?' she persisted. '*We* only just know— we've only just left the hospital!'

'Clearly someone has leaked the information—it could be anyone.'

She looked at his profile—how could he not be furious? 'Isn't medical information meant to be private and confidential?'

'I protect my privacy as well as I can, but in this instance I see no reason to be overly concerned.'

'I'm surprised they haven't announced our marriage.'

'They didn't need to—I put an announcement in the papers.'

'You did what?' Horrified, Sam buried her face in her hands and groaned.

'Is that a problem? I had no idea it was meant to be a secret.'

Her head came up at the frosty note of annoyance in his voice. 'Yes, it is a problem. What if my family read it? I haven't told them yet, remember?'

'Ah!'

'Exactly!'

'I hadn't thought about that one,' he admitted.

'You must be slipping,' she retorted, gnawing reflectively on her lower lip as she considered how best to soothe her brother's injured feelings.

'I'll speak to your brother if you like... explain things.'

Sam politely refused the offer.

The information she intended to give her over-protective brother was going to be carefully censored. The last thing she wanted was Cesare giving a full and frank account.

When they did reach home Cesare raised no objections when Sam banished him from their bedroom so that she could speak to her relations, even though he had had a very different idea of how to celebrate his bill of clean health.

It was after he left her that he had an excellent idea.

Snatching up a jacket, he informed the housekeeper that he was going out and that if his wife asked tell her he'd be back very soon.

To Sam's utter relief it turned out that neither Ian nor Clare had read the offending announcement.

The conversation was not that easy, partly because at first Ian was inclined to consider her statement that she was married to an Italian billionaire a wind-up.

'Sure you are, Sam,' Ian drawled. 'So what have you actually been up to, little sister?'

When she did convince him she was not joking Ian's response was far from encouraging.

'Are you insane, Sam?'

'Why is it insane for me to get married?'

'You mean beyond the fact you barely know the man? For starters, he is a multibillionaire or something.'

'Clare was the daughter of a laird, you were the son of the grocer. I'm not marrying him for his money.'

'God knows, I wish you had that much sense!' her brother exploded, sounding exasperated. 'How in God's name did you meet him to begin with?'

Sam kept her reply deliberately vague. 'He was slumming it and we…'

There was genuine anxiety in her brother's voice as he said, 'This guy lives in a world we know nothing about, Sam.'

'I'm learning.'

'Didn't he date that gorgeous actress for a while?'

'What you're struggling so hard *not* to say is I'm not a film star or glamorous.'

'You're nice-looking enough in your own way.'

This brotherly tribute brought a wry smile to Sam's lips.

'Has the explanation that he might love me occurred to you?'

The silence said it hadn't.

'Will it help you fathom out the attraction if—?'

Ian interrupted, sounding irritated. 'For God's sake, what am I meant to say? He'll get bored with you in a month!' There was a pause before he added apologetically, 'Well, I'm sorry, Sam, but it's a fact.'

Sam's teeth grated. 'How is it a fact? Because you say so? How dare you judge Cesare?' she said, her voice quivering with outrage. 'You know nothing about him but what you read in the press.'

There was a lengthy pause after her heated defence.

'Obviously I hope I am wrong.'

Then she blurted, 'I'm pregnant, Ian!' and his response almost blasted her eardrums into oblivion.

When he had finished telling her that she had made the worst mistake of her life he handed her over to Clare, who did much the same thing only a lot more tactfully and with offers of support and enquiries about the baby thrown in.

* * *

Sam was feeling quite depressed and her self-esteem was at an all-time low when she put the phone down. Her mood was not uplifted when the housekeeper informed her that, not only had Cesare left the house, but she had a visitor.

When Sam enquired after the visitor's identity Mrs Havers pursed her lips in tight disapproval.

'It's that actress, Candice Royal. I said you weren't at home, but she barged in as bold as you like acting as if the place was her own, which she thought it would be…and I don't mind telling you if it had I'd have been out of the door…but…' The older woman appeared to realise that she was being indiscreet and called a halt to her diatribe.

'Did she come to see Cesare or…?'

'Yes.'

The fear that Sam felt was quickly followed by anger.

How dared this woman come here? She had to know that Cesare was newly married. Was she coming to cause trouble or was this a let's-all-be-friends visit?

Maybe that was the civilised way to go about

things, but Sam wasn't feeling very civilised. At that precise moment some very uncivilised thoughts were passing through her head.

'Paolo is in his flat—I could get him to come up and turf her out?'

Sam partially shared the housekeeper's obvious enthusiasm to see the actress bodily removed from the house, but shook her head.

If it was anyone's job to show the woman the door, it was Cesare's. But maybe he wouldn't want to?

Sam knew her pregnancy wasn't detectable yet, but she was entering the stage where she felt she simply looked fat. However, she had been encouraged by Cesare's comments to think that he had no problem with the idea of her expanding girth.

The moment she laid eyes on the unexpected visitor in the drawing room she lost the glow of confidence his admiration had given her. In the presence of this stunning blonde with the endless legs and the tiny waist she felt like a small, scruffy mongrel.

In which case Cesare's ex-fiancée was a tall, elegant Afghan. The older woman was wearing a white tailored trouser suit cinched in at the waist and cut low across a gravity defying bosom.

She forced a smile. 'Hello. Have you been waiting long? Would you like tea? Mrs Havers…?'

The housekeeper, who had entered the room in Sam's wake gave an acquiescent nod and, with a look of rigid disapproval in the direction of their guest, turned to go.

Candice smiled sympathetically and commented in a voice clearly intended to carry, 'Good help is hard to get these days.'

'I really can't let you speak badly of a fellow Scot,' Sam said, taking the sting out of her words with another smile. 'Actually, Mrs Havers has been marvellous helping me settle in.'

Candice raised a brow at the robust defence. 'I don't suppose you know anything about being mistress of a large establishment. You do realise that this place is small compared to the Tuscan Castillo? And the New York apartment is magnificent—the décor was done by—'

It didn't take a genius to see that the other woman was trying to make Sam feel like the outsider and she succeeded pretty well. But Sam decided two could play at that game.

'Actually Cesare is thinking of selling the New York apartment and getting something a bit more child friendly…Cape Cod, we'd thought,' she lied fluently.

'Yes, I heard you were pregnant. But I really can't see Cesare with a family.'

Sam's smile grew fixed. If she had anything to do with it Candice wouldn't be seeing Cesare at all. She lifted her brows and evinced surprise. 'Really? He never mentioned to you he wants five?'

A look of horror settled over the other woman's face.

'Cesare wants five children?'

'I said four was enough. What do you think?'

'Oh, I'm no expert on children, but I adore my little Eduardo.'

Sam assumed that she was speaking of a nephew until she lifted the lid of the bag she carried and the small head of a tiny dog emerged with bows tied in its carefully groomed curls.

'That's why it surprises me that Cesare wants

babies. He never liked little Eduardo—he was actually quite cruel to him.'

'How strange,' Sam said, holding back the laughter.

'And he's very sensitive, aren't you? Mummy's little darling,' the actress crooned before closing the lid on the poor unfortunate creature with a click and saying, 'There's been a spate of dog-nappings in the area but I never let Eduardo out of my sight.'

'Very wise. Shall I ask Mrs Havers to bring some water for him?'

'What brand?'

Sam stared and realised Candice was being deadly serious. 'I'm not sure. Shall I ask Mrs Havers?'

'Thank you, but he's fine for now. I wouldn't put it past that woman to bring him tap water. You know, I virtually had to push past her when I arrived, even though she knew who I was, but never mind that.' She dismissed the subject of the housekeeper and treated Sam to a searching scrutiny. 'You're much bigger than I imagined.'

Sam got the feeling she was talking width-ways.

'Have you booked your personal trainer yet for afterwards…?'

Sam met the blonde's gaze evenly. 'I hadn't really considered having one.'

'Not have a trainer!' She gasped, looking totally baffled. 'How will you get back into shape?'

'Gradually, I expect, and looking after a baby will be something of a full-time job, at least at first.'

'My friend says the trick is to have a night nurse and a nanny and…'

Sam laughed and watched a look of shock spread across the other woman's face as she explained she wasn't going to have a nanny.'

'Is there something I can do for you, Miss…?'

'Call me Candice. I had hoped that Cesare would be with you.' She pouted her disappointment. 'But, oh, well…' With a smile and a motion of her lovely hand that sent the bangles on her narrow wrist jingling against the gold of her tanned skin, Candice waved Sam to a seat opposite her.

As if *she* were the visitor, Sam thought, taking a seat at the opposite side of the low table. Her facial muscles were aching with the effort of maintaining a smile.

'It's probably better if you and I have a private chat first.'

Sam couldn't think of anything less enjoyable than a private chat with the love of Cesare's life. She turned as the housekeeper returned carrying a tea tray. Laying it down on the table beside Sam, Mrs Havers said pointedly, 'I'm just outside.'

Sam smiled her thanks and said, 'I'll be fine.'

When the door closed Candice leaned forward in a confidential manner, revealing in the process the fact she wasn't wearing a stitch beneath the tailored jacket. 'Is it true?' she asked in a voice that throbbed with emotion, which Sam decided was fake.

Sam's wooden smile stayed in place as she studied the actress and felt something approaching rage stir deep inside. Before she had met her she had felt guilty for harbouring pretty nasty thoughts about the beautiful woman whom Cesare had wanted to marry, who had been his first choice, but now she had met her she no longer felt that guilt.

The woman more than justified a few nasty thoughts—and Cesare had terrible taste! So what if the woman was even more beautiful in real life than on screen? That her skin was like porcelain and her figure voluptuous? She oozed insincerity through every perfect pore. She was selfish and self-centred and…oh, God, Sam thought, stifling a groan, there was no way in the world she could compete with her!

'Is what true?'

'Has Cesare recovered his sight?'

Sam nodded, wondering where this was going. 'Yes, he has.'

A sigh shuddered through the other woman as she leaned back in her seat and crossed one shapely ankle across the other. 'Thank God!' she breathed, dabbing at the corners of her dry eyes with a tissue. 'I'm sorry, but you have no idea what this means to me…You know, of course, that we were engaged. Has he told you why we…?'

'Cesare has never spoken of you to me, but I assumed that—'

'That I left him after the accident…' She gave a small laugh. 'Yes, that's what everyone thought, but actually it was Cesare who ended it. He said he loved me too much to burden me with a husband who had a disability. Of course, I tried to dissuade him, but he said it would not be fair.'

'How noble,' Sam said drily.

'Cesare is my soul mate,' Candice stated in a throbbing tone that Sam found as fake as her surgically enhanced breasts.

And I'm his wife, Sam thought, compressing her lips.

She kept her expression impassive. The critic who had savaged the actress's last film and suggested sarcastically that Candice Royal couldn't act herself out of a paper bag had not been wrong.

This realisation was small comfort when Sam recalled that the critic had also admitted that most of his own sex would forgive Candice this total lack of talent because she looked so good with her top off—something she apparently spent a lot of time doing in that film.

'So now you see,' Candice started to say before she stopped and lifted a hand to her heaving and, if the critic was to be believed, pretty stupendous bosom, 'why the news of his recovery affected me so much.'

A couple of sniffs did not seem a particularly strong reaction to Sam, but she maintained her silence. The older woman appeared not to notice her lack of response, but then she was probably the sort of woman who liked to have centre stage.

'You can have no idea how I'm feeling… now, of course, nothing stands in the way of us being together.'

'I beg your pardon?'

'The only reason we split up was his ridiculous scruples, so now there is nothing in the way of our happiness.'

Sam stared. This woman was unbelievable! 'Other than a wife and child,' she said, touching a shaking hand to her belly.

'This must be hard for you—I'm sure you care about Cesare in your own way….'

Sam got slowly to her feet, her knees feeling like jelly. 'I *love* Cesare,' she corrected, pressing a clenched hand to her chest. 'I love him the way a wife loves her husband.'

Candice looked momentarily taken aback by the vehemence of Sam's hissing retort. Then she smiled.

'If you love him, then I'm sure you want him to be happy.'

Sam lifted her chin. 'He is happy.'

She caught her quivering lower lip between her teeth. She could hear the defiance in her voice and from the flicker in the other woman's green eyes she knew that Candice had heard it too.

Candice's manner was that of someone who could afford to be generous as she said comfortingly, 'Oh, I'm sure he pretends to be happy, but, well, think about it…'

'Think about what?' Sam asked, as if she didn't know what the actress could be talking about. But she did know. She had seen women look at Cesare, have the usual salivating reaction, and then look at her. Sam could almost see what they were thinking—how on earth did *she* get him?

'I don't mean to be cruel.'

The comment dragged Sam's wandering thoughts back to her visitor.

'Pardon?'

The smile with zero warmth returned. 'I don't mean to be cruel.'

Like a cat didn't mean to torture its prey.

Sam tightened her jaw and gathered her defences around her tightly like a cloak.

If she was going to fall apart, and at the moment it seemed pretty inevitable she would at some point, it would not be in front of this woman.

One hand across her belly, she leaned across and poured milk into her teacup. Not because she had any intention of drinking anything—her stomach was churning—but to give herself space to regain a little composure. Then, forcing her lips back into a smile, she slipped off her shoes and tucked her legs underneath her.

As she received one of Sam's candid stares the other woman's air of confident self-possession wavered slightly.

'But you're going to be cruel anyway?' Sam suggested.

Candice's green eyes narrowed. 'Are you the sort of woman that catches the like of Cesare Brunelli…?' Her tinkling laugh invited Sam to share the joke.

Sam didn't smile. She opened her mouth to refute the suggestion and found she couldn't. How could she? It was true.

'Let's face it, he's out of your league.'

'You don't know me or anything about me, let alone what league I play in.'

'You play in the nice person's league,' Cesare's ex observed with a smile that sent angry colour flying to Sam's cheeks. 'You are nice.'

And she was sure Candice was not, Sam thought. What on earth had Cesare seen in her, other than the obvious?

'But Cesare is a man, and men are not interested in the personality or niceness of the woman he is seen with. A man in Cesare's position needs to present a certain image to the world and his wife is part of that image.'

'A trophy wife.'

The other woman shrugged. 'If you like.'

A few months before, when Cesare Brunelli was just a headline to her, Sam might have endorsed this view without question. She might even have said much the same herself if asked to give her opinion of the Italian billionaire!

But now things were different. 'In my experience Cesare doesn't give a damn about what anyone thinks of him.'

Candice looked irritated by her obstinacy. 'I think I know Cesare a little better than you.'

'Do you *really* think that Cesare is that shallow?'

For the first time the blonde lost her air of patronising calm. Her lips were tight as she snapped, 'He's a man.'

A man who had squeezed Sam's fingers so tight as she had described the image of his unborn child to him that she had winced. No, the man she had married was many things, but shallow was not one of them.

Sam spoke her next statement with confidence. 'You're not in love with Cesare, are you? I don't think you even like him.'

'The point is he isn't in love with you, is he? That's not why he married you. You trapped him.'

'Has it occurred to you that maybe I'm just hot in bed?'

It was obvious from the other woman's outraged, shocked expression that she had not.

'Maybe he married me for sex,' Sam continued.

'I consider that joke to be very bad taste.'

'I wouldn't open up the subject of good taste if I was wearing that jacket and no bra. And who says I'm joking?' she added belligerently.

The blonde pursed her carmine tinted glossy lips. 'I'm sure you realise that had he not been blind you would never have caught him.'

It was only pride that stopped Sam flinching in reaction to this calculated cruelty. 'I was not trying to catch him.'

'You got pregnant.'

'Not on my own.'

The blonde sucked in a startled breath of outrage through her clenched teeth and rose with ruffled dignity to her feet.

Sam did likewise and felt at an immediate disadvantage. Her body felt squat next to the slender elegance of the actress.

'I made the effort. I wanted this to be amicable.'

'You're acting as if it's a foregone conclusion that Cesare will dump me for you.'

The blonde shook back her mane of silky straight hair and laughed. 'All I have to do is—' She clicked her fingers.

Sam cut angrily across her. 'Then go do it,' she advised, 'because I'm not giving up without a fight.'

CHAPTER TWELVE

By THE time Sam heard Cesare's voice in the hallway an hour later she'd decided she wasn't only going to give him his divorce, she was going to *insist* on it.

She might have put on a good act in front of Candice, but she didn't want to be any man's consolation prize. He could have Candice and good riddance. She was not going to compete for the favours of any man.

'And I hope they make each other miserable!' she gritted through clenched teeth.

But when he walked into the drawing room thirty seconds later her opinion had undergone another lightning change of direction. Why should she give him his freedom so easily? Why should she make things easy for him and that horrific woman?

She owed it to their child to at least put up a fight. Besides, as annoying as Cesare was, she really thought he deserved more than the shallow, conniving blonde.

It took Cesare about two seconds to deduce that all was not well. If the tear stains were not conclusive, the stormy look in Sam's violet eyes was—she was mad as hell and that anger appeared to be directed at him.

'Oh, you finally decided to put in an appearance, then. I suppose I should be grateful?'

Cesare studied the colour on her cheeks and the glow in her eyes and smiled. If the audible grating of her teeth was an indicator, she appeared to find the smile provocative.

'What have I done?' he asked, thinking about how she had looked when she had woken this morning, her hair on the pillow, her face sleepily flushed.

'Nothing. Absolutely nothing,' Sam muttered. She just loved entertaining his mistress.

When Cesare angled his head and looked down at her through the sweep of his dark lashes Sam ran her tongue across her dry lips, perplexed by his enigmatic expression and not quite sure what to say next. Any version of her pre-rehearsed speech had gone from her head the moment he'd walked in.

She glared at him some more and waited while he brushed an invisible speck off his trousers. Then he smiled the lopsided smile that always made her stomach flip.

She watched as he picked up a book off a bureau and ran his finger down the spine. He put it back down with exaggerated care before he crossed the room towards her in a handful of long-legged, elegant strides.

'I feel like I've walked into the middle of a scene.' He arched a dark brow sardonically and folded his arms across his chest. 'Would you like to fill in the gaps for me, *cara*?'

The softness of his enquiry did not fool Sam for a second. She could see he was annoyed with her. 'While you were out I decided to offer you a divorce.'

His eyes narrowed instantly, but the expression in the dark depths was frustratingly inscrutable. 'You have my attention.'

It was hard to think when his eyes were trained like lasers on her face. 'I don't want your attention, I want…'

He angled an enquiring brow and, biting her lip, she turned her head away.

'A divorce?' he suggested, thinking how hell would freeze over before he would let that happen. 'Considering we have only just returned from our honeymoon, do you not feel that this is a little premature? And what makes you think I would accept such an offer?'

Sam gave an offhand shrug. 'It doesn't matter I changed my mind.' The pulsating silence couldn't have lasted more than a heartbeat but Sam couldn't bear it. 'So tough!' she rasped.

'Am I meant to know what I have done?' Despite his conversational tone, Sam could feel the waves of tension rolling off his lean body.

'Don't take that tone with me!' she retorted angrily.

He closed the remaining distance between them, moving with a fluidity and grace that had the power to make her stomach flip in appreciation even in this moment of extreme emotional stress.

His lean, dark face set in a mask of dark fury, he towered over her and enquired with biting politeness, 'I'm curious, *cara*—what tone am I meant to take when I arrive home and my wife announces she intends to offer me a divorce?' He angled a brow and studied her face with grim intensity. 'Have you any idea what that feels like?'

Sam's hands balled into fists and, raising them, she brought them against his chest with a thud. The moment she made contact with the hard surface her anger dissolved into misery.

A choking sob was dragged from her throat as her chin dropped to her chest.

'Samantha…?'

Unable to force a response past the aching constriction in her throat, she shook her head. Her fingers opened and she clutched at the fabric of his shirt, feeling the warmth of his body.

He slid his long fingers into her hair, lifting it off her neck. When she felt his breath warm against her skin, it prickled as though an electrical current had passed through her body.

'Don't,' she whispered.

'Don't what?'

Her knees sagged and he wrapped a supporting arm around her ribcage, hauling her to him.

Sam lifted her teary eyes to his. Her pupils
were dilated, her lips quivering. She sniffed
loudly and said, 'I'm not happy.'

Cesare felt her words like a knife to the heart,
an organ that had never caused him pain previously. Like him it had been living in an emotional vacuum. A muscle along his jaw clenched
as he silently vowed that he would do whatever
it took to make the person who was responsible
for waking his heart from hibernation happy.

Even if that means letting her go?

Cesare, the first to admit he was a man, not a
saint, refused to contemplate this possibility. The
thought of any other man touching her made his
blood roar with rage.

'I will change.'

The raw emotion in his voice as much as his
words brought her head up. 'I…'

His hands tightened around her waist. 'You
don't think I can?' he challenged as his eyes
claimed Sam's.

The burning intensity in his bottomless black

searching stare made Sam's head spin dizzily. 'I think you can do anything if you want to,' she said honestly. 'Why would you want to change?' He seemed to her about as perfect as it got and he wouldn't be Cesare if he weren't ridiculously proud and too stubborn for his own good.

'I'm making you unhappy.' His lean face contorted in self-disgust as he released her and his hands fell from her waist.

Sam watched, wishing he hadn't let her go and utterly confused by the strong emotions surrounding him like an aura.

She wrapped her arms in a protective gesture around herself and shivered. She'd spent her entire life standing on her own feet, so why was it that being in love made her feel so damned weak and needy?

Cesare inhaled through flared nostrils drawing air into his lungs and dragging a hand through his dark hair that had begun to curl onto his collar. It reminded her of the way it had been when she had first seen him.

'We can work through this,' he said, adopting a tone of calm reason that might have been more convincing if it hadn't been for the muscles clenching and unclenching like a time bomb in his hollow cheek.

'You want to work through it?'

The façade of calm reason slipped as he gritted through clenched teeth, 'Of course I want to work it through. Why else would I say—?' He stopped, visibly calling upon his reserves of self-control. 'Yes, I want to work it through. The first item on the agenda…'

A slightly hysterical laugh was wrenched from Sam's throat. 'Shall I take minutes?'

His dark brows drew into a disapproving line above his smouldering eyes.

Sam lowered her own gaze and whispered, 'Sorry.'

'Why are you unhappy?'

The question brought her eyes back up. Suddenly she was so angry with him she wanted to scream. 'Why do you think?'

Before he could respond to her furious question she pointed an accusing finger at him and yelled, 'You ask me if I know what it feels like and *you*—!' She broke off, shaking her head as the strength of her indignation momentarily robbed her of speech.

His heavy-lidded eyes narrowed as he struggled to rein in his impatience and a growing sense of desperation. '*Per amor di Dio*. What have I done?'

She sucked in a deep breath and fixed him with a smouldering blue glare. 'I'll tell you what you've done,' she promised grimly, before answering. 'Have *you* any idea what it feels like to have *your ex* arrive and explain that she didn't dump you because of the accident, and that *you* ended things?'

A look of genuine shock relaxed the lines of angry tension in his lean face. 'Candice?'

As far as Cesare knew she was still travelling with the Argentinian polo player she had become inseparable from after their split.

Sam vented a bitter little laugh. 'Have you any other exes?'

'Candice came to see you?' He shook his dark head and looked blank. Of all the things he had anticipated her saying this had never even crossed his mind.

Sam's lips tightened, his manner jarred on her. For a man who was normally several mental leaps ahead of the field he seemed to be being particularly dense, although the vacant look of incomprehension might be his way of concealing his feelings for his ex from her.

Maybe the mention of Candice's name made his heart rate quicken? Did he suffer the agonising pangs of helpless craving in the pit of his stomach when he thought about her? Was he empty and aching inside without her?

The intensity of the stab of jealousy that shot through her drew a pained gasp from her chest.

Concern in his eyes, Cesare reached out, but Sam backed away, batting at his hand. Her dark feathery brows drew together above her shimmering eyes as she levelled an unfriendly glare at him.

'*Did* you end the engagement?' she asked, thinking, *Say no...say no...*please *say no!*

Cesare shrugged and confirmed, 'I did end it.'

Sam expelled a shaky sigh as her narrow shoulders slumped. She felt totally deflated emotionally. Her last hope had evaporated. 'So she was telling the truth?'

'There is, I suppose, a first time for everything.'

Sam looked at him blankly, barely registering his comment. Barely registering anything but the wild conflict of turbulent emotions churning inside her.

He studied the tragic face upturned to him, let out a curse and took hold of her shoulders. 'Just what truth did Candice tell you, Samantha?'

Sam, struggling to adopt an expression of nonchalant disinterest, shook her head a little and the action made the tension in her throbbing temples ratchet up another painful notch.

'She told me that you wouldn't marry her because you wouldn't burden the woman you love with your disability.'

A look of blank astonishment crossed Cesare's face as he froze.

'She said that you only married me because of the baby…which, of course, you did, but actually,' she admitted, 'it wasn't all that nice to hear it. She said that if you hadn't been blind you wouldn't have slept with me in the first place… right again…'

There was a pulsating pause before Cesare responded, before he trusted himself to respond. 'Candice appears to have said entirely too much and *you* appear to have believed every word.'

The condemnatory comment struck Sam as too unjust. 'I did think it strange that you never mentioned her. Now I know why,' she said bitterly.

'You know nothing,' he contradicted grimly. 'And the reason I never mentioned Candice is because she is not important. She is the past.'

'You admitted—' she began, only to be cut off by him.

'Admitted?' He raised a brow and felt his temper rise. 'Does this mean I am on trial?' He shook his head in disbelief. 'You're the one who told me what a selfish waste of space I am. I'm amazed you think me capable of such noble self-sacrifice,' he drawled sarcastically. 'It may have escaped your notice, but I thought I would be blind for the rest of my life when I asked you to marry me. I had no qualms about tying you to a blind man for life.'

If Sam had not been so utterly wretched and miserable she would have found Cesare's steely black stare unnerving. 'You said marriage does not have to be for ever.'

'I would not say anything so ludicrous.'

'But you did!'

His shoulders lifted in a shrug. 'Well, maybe I did,' he acknowledged with obvious reluctance. 'But that comment was meant as a general observation. I was not speaking about our situation. Other people can divorce, they do not interest me. For us marriage is for ever.'

'And,' Sam added, warming to her theme of resentment, 'you didn't ask me, you *told* me we were getting married.' Sam sniffed and searched her pocket for a tissue... She would not cry; she would not beg. She couldn't make someone love her.

Cesare conceded the correction with a fluid shrug and a lopsided smile.

'And you're not in love with me,' Sam declared. Her bright smile had a heartbreaking quality. 'You only married me because of the baby and I'm fine with that.' She stopped and looked through her lashes at his dark, strangely still face. 'Well, no, I'm not fine with it, but I accept that's the way things are.' The admission hurt her soul-deep.

She expelled a shaky breath and lifted a hand to her head.

Cesare took her face between his hands.

'Well, I cannot accept things the way they are,' he admitted.

The last remaining colour seeped from her skin.

Cesare carried on speaking. 'I did break up with Candice, but not after the accident.'

Sam blinked and shook her head. 'I don't understand.'

'I ended my relationship with Candice two weeks before the accident,' he revealed harshly.

'But Candice…'

'Candice has a very…flexible relationship with the truth. We parted the day I discovered she had been sleeping with someone else while I was away on a business trip.'

Sam's eyes widened with shock.

'You want to know how that made me feel?'

Knowing how his heart had been torn out by another woman was actually not very high on the list of things Sam wished to hear about. Her glance slid from his. 'Betrayed, hurt, humiliated…?' she suggested.

'No, I felt relieved.'

Her eyes lifted and a frown formed on her smooth brow as she studied his face. 'Relieved?'

Cesare nodded. 'Yes, relieved, because it made things simpler. I already knew that I was never going to marry Candice. I was not under any illusions concerning her feelings for me. The love of Candice's life is and will always be the current designer handbag that everyone who is anyone wants to be seen carrying. She is a pragmatic woman and the lifespan of an actress whose sole talent lies in being photographed wearing outrageous outfits is limited. I was the means for her to go on buying the bags.'

'But why on earth were you going to marry her?'

'I confess that my motivation was just as selfish and trivial as hers.' He made a grimace of distaste. 'The only time I've thought of Candice since I met you was when you reminded me I'd said that marriage was not permanent. When I got engaged to her it never even crossed my mind that we would grow old together. It was convenient. I had lost interest in the chase. All women seemed the same to me and Candice's publicity people had been dropping hints the size of Wales about an engagement. When a magazine approached me for a confirmation or denial I made the mistake of giving an ironic response. People who work on those sort of magazines have a slender grasp of irony.'

'You could have denied it.'

'I could and I obviously should have,' he agreed. 'But I suppose if I'm honest I had this uncomfortable feeling that I might one day turn into my father.' His revulsion at the prospect was easy to see in his face. 'Like him I'd had my share of shallow relationships and I thought if I was going to get married it might as well be with someone as cold as me, someone I couldn't hurt because I was unable to share their feelings.'

'You're not cold!' she protested huskily.

His eyes softened with warmth that made her breath catch. '*Cara*, before I met you I had developed cynicism into an art form. As for Candice, I had no high expectations of her, but I did not expect her to jump into bed with other men every time I was out of the country.'

Sam winced.

'So when I walked in one day and found her in bed with some pretty actor I decided to cut my losses. I didn't much care when she spread the story that she had dumped me, though when I had the accident the lie backfired on her with a vengeance.'

'I don't understand.'

'The timing was not good. People assumed that she had dumped me because she couldn't stomach a husband with a disability. She became box-office poison.'

'It couldn't happen to a nicer person.'

This evidence of her jealousy brought a broad smile tinged with a mixture of smugness and relief to Cesare's face.

'You know, you may not realise it now but you are in love with me.'

Sam regarded him with fascination. 'You think so?'

'I know so,' he corrected with a full measure of the infuriating arrogance she knew she would actually miss if he turned humble overnight.

'You're wrong, you know. I do realise it. I've realised for a long time that I adore you even if you are the most stubborn, infuriating man alive. I love you, Cesare.'

There were seconds of shattered silence before he gave a hoarse groan and brought his mouth crashing down on hers. He kissed her until her head was spinning and when he stopped kissing her he stood holding her, looking into her face as if it was the most perfect thing he had ever seen.

He slowly trailed a finger down the side of her cheek before expelling a shaky breath and gathering her to him, into the shelter of his hard body. He cupped her chin in one hand and pressed his nose against hers so their breaths mingled.

'My feelings for you, Samantha…'

'You have feelings for me?' she asked innocently. His feelings for her were a subject Sam was more than happy to explore.

'How can you ask me that? I couldn't put a name to them because they were feelings I had never had before. I didn't know what love was. I didn't recognise it even when it was right there in front of me. Every time I heard your voice, felt your touch… When I could not see I would lie there imagining your face…your beautiful face. And when I said it…I knew, Samantha.'

The raw emotion in his voice touched her soul-deep.

'When you lifted that veil, you took my breath away. I didn't know which way up I was standing. I was finally able to recognise my feelings for what they were—I was in love.

'You saved me, Samantha. I managed to push everyone who cared for me away and everyone else was too scared to tell me what a total coward I was being—everyone except you.

'You brought the light back into my life. You were, you are,' he corrected thickly, 'the light in my life. I was in a dark place and you arrived like a bolt of lightning—almost literally. You're amazing,' he marveled, tracing the line of her jaw. 'You look so delicate but you're so tough and brave. You have a generosity of spirit that my cynical soul didn't want to believe in. I tried not to, even after you gave me your body. I told myself it was just sex, but even then I knew it was more.'

Samantha was weeping openly by this point. 'I don't want your gratitude, Cesare.'

'Well, you have it anyway, *cara*, and with it my love. You might not want that either, but it is yours.' He took one of her small hands in his brown fingers, interweaving them as he laid it against his chest. 'As is my heart.'

Sam closed her eyes. She could feel the heavy thud of his steady heartbeat. Her hand lay on his heart, but it was Cesare who was reaching out to her with his defences down. Inside her, joy exploded like a star burst. 'I accept it, Cesare.'

'Oh, and this too,' he said, releasing her hand to delve in the pocket of his trousers from which he withdrew a slim velvet box. 'I'm not trying to buy your love,' he said as he handed it to her. 'But I wanted to give you something that expressed what I couldn't.'

'You haven't done so badly,' she said huskily as she slipped the clasp and lifted the lid. Inside lay a necklace, a string of sapphires in a delicate gold old-fashioned Victorian setting.

'I wanted to do something for you that I have never done for another woman. I've always delegated the task,' he admitted shamefacedly. 'I've never bought a gift for a woman. I know it's not the crown jewels and if those are what you want, *cara*, I will buy or steal them for you. But the colour, the glorious depth, they just made me think of your lovely eyes.'

She saw the message glowing in his midnight eyes through a teary glaze. A soft sigh rippled through her as the last of her doubts vanished.

'They are beautiful, Cesare.'

'The idea of me losing my sight again terrified me, but it did not even begin to come close to the terror I feel at the thought of losing you, Samantha.'

She took his hand and fitted it around her softly rounded belly. 'You're not going to lose me or this one, Cesare,' she promised, her eyes shining with the depth of her love.

EPILOGUE

IT WAS a year and six months later that they were getting ready for the glittering gala event at the Venetian palazzo of a friend of Cesare's.

Sam had tiptoed out of the room where their one-year-old daughter, Natalia, lay asleep when Cesare walked around the corner demanding in a loud voice where she had put his cufflinks.

'Shush!' Sam urged with a nervous grimace. 'She's just fallen asleep. I've already done the teddy story three times complete with actions. Another and I think I might break.'

'Well, you'll just have to write the next instalment, *cara.*'

'Because I've got so much time on my hands?' she suggested with an ironic twinkle. Since she'd given birth the previous year, Sam had barely had a moment to call her own. Cesare, unbeknownst to her, had presented the children's story she had kept in a drawer to a publisher and to her amazement it had been accepted. She had been called upon to spend several weeks publicising it, which, when you were nursing a new baby, required some logistical skill and stamina.

The problem was—if success could be called that—her teddy story had not just pleased her daughter, it had pleased hundreds of thousands of other children and it wasn't just Cesare who was suggesting she produce a second volume, it was the publishers who were urging her to have another go.

Being Cesare's wife was almost a full-time job in itself and being an active member of a charity aiming to reduce adult illiteracy also kept her busy. But she knew that over the next few months she might find her energy reserves depleted— and it was a subject she needed to discuss with her husband very soon.

Distracted from his cufflink search by the sight of his wife resplendent in a Grecian-inspired dress that revealed one smooth shoulder, Cesare let out a silent whistle and gave a mock leer.

'Wow, you look incredible, *cara mia*!'

Sam grinned and said, 'You don't look so bad yourself.' His shirt was unbuttoned to the waist, revealing his taut muscled torso, and looking at his body sent a familiar wave of heat through her.

Sam backed away laughing as he reached for her.

'Have you any idea how long it took to get my hair like this?' she said, shaking her head and causing a rippling effect in the artfully casual arrangement of curling tendrils that framed her face.

'I'm pretty sure it wouldn't take me long to mess it,' Cesare observed with a grin.

'That's what I'm worried about,' she retorted.

'Those cufflinks, Sam…'

She released a sigh. 'Caught out again—I've been wearing them…'

'Funny lady,' he said walking towards the open door of their daughter's room. 'I won't wake her,' he promised, tiptoeing to the bed where the sleeping figure was illuminated by the glow of a night light.

Sam walked up behind him and stood with him looking down at their rosy-faced daughter.

Cesare's arms came around her and she leaned back into him with a sigh.

'She's a wonder, isn't she?' he said softly. 'The second most beautiful thing in the world,' he whispered, kissing the top of Sam's glossy head. 'And the fact I nearly lost you both makes her all the more precious,' he finished heavily.

'You didn't nearly lose us,' she scoffed, rubbing her face against his muscled arm. 'Thousands of women have a Caesarean. It's no big deal.' Though admittedly it had felt it at the time. She had clung onto Cesare's hand so hard when they had said the baby's heart rate had dropped that he had had the bruises for weeks.

'An *emergency* Caesarean,' he corrected. 'And it is a big deal, a very big deal when it is my women. You know that night took at least ten years off my life!'

'Never mind—this time the Caesarean will be scheduled. At least it will be if the next baby is as big as this little elephant was. I've not got the pelvis for a big baby.'

'Me, I am particularly fond of your pelvis,' he said, playfully slapping her rear.

Sam spun around and tilted her head up to him in mock reproach. 'That,' she said, wagging her finger, 'is not my pelvis.'

'No, but it too is very nice indeed.' He stopped dead. 'You said *this* time…'

Sam took a deep breath. 'I did.'

His eyes dropped to her stomach and he swallowed. 'Does that mean…?'

She nodded. 'I'm ten weeks. Are you happy?' She angled an anxious look at his dark face, but there was nothing much to read in it other than stunned shock. Though she had joked about Natalia's birth, she was well aware of how deeply Cesare had been affected by her tough and prolonged labour. 'I know we weren't planning another just yet and after last time you said you couldn't go through that again, but…?'

'Happy?' He took her face between his hands. 'Before I had you and our baby I thought I was happy. I slept well and I never thought about what could have happened. I never felt a stab of sheer terror all for the simple reason I didn't have anything in my life that I couldn't have replaced.' He shook his head, amazed that he had survived so long without any centre to his life. 'My girls are totally irreplaceable, two perfect jewels.'

The husky declaration brought a rush of tears to her eyes. 'Oh, God, if you make me cry—' she sniffed '—I'll never forgive you. It took me hours to look this good.'

'Now I'm happy!' he said, placing the flat of her hand on his chest. 'My heart is alive and life is painful, true, but, God, it's so sweet. I'll be terrified every second until this new baby is born,' he admitted, 'but this time I'll be better prepared. I've already done some research so that when the time comes—'

'You can tell the medics what they're doing wrong,' she cut in with a grin. 'I can see you're going to be really popular.' And she could see how this strategy might work for her husband, who did not like relinquishing control. 'So as you've *already* done research, is it possible you've been thinking never might be a long time to wait for another baby?' she teased.

A smile glimmered in his eyes. 'It has crossed

my mind once or twice,' he admitted. 'Even if it means more grey hairs.'

Sam laughed as she lifted a hand to his pure sable head. 'You don't have any grey hairs.'

'But I will,' he predicted. And it seemed to him a small price for the love of this woman whom he could not imagine life without. 'And will you still love me then?'

'I will never stop loving you, Cesare, though obviously if you lost your hair…' She let her voice trail off and sighed. 'A girl has to draw the line somewhere.'

'And so,' added Cesare firmly, 'does a man. And I draw the line at sharing you with anyone else tonight,' he decided. 'Besides, if you arrive looking like that you will break too many hearts. Shall we stay home?'

Sam found the offer tempting. 'Won't Draco be hurt if we don't turn up?'

'Forget about Draco and think about me,' Cesare said, grabbing her by her waist and kissing her deeply.

Sam emerged from the kiss with a dreamy smile on her face. 'I never stop thinking about you, Cesare.' She gave a deep sigh of contentment. 'Actually, when you think about it a man can't be expected to attend an event without his favourite cufflinks… I'm sure Draco would understand.'

'Draco will understand perfectly,' Cesare agreed, bending his head once more to kiss her. 'I think he's half in love with you himself, but he knows you're my girl.'

Sam smiled. She had found rare joy and she intended to never stop reminding herself of the fact she was the luckiest girl alive—she was Cesare's girl.

MILLS & BOON PUBLISH EIGHT LARGE PRINT TITLES A MONTH. THESE ARE THE EIGHT TITLES FOR AUGUST 2009.

THE SPANISH BILLIONAIRE'S PREGNANT WIFE
Lynne Graham

THE ITALIAN'S RUTHLESS MARRIAGE COMMAND
Helen Bianchin

THE BRUNELLI BABY BARGAIN
Kim Lawrence

THE FRENCH TYCOON'S PREGNANT MISTRESS
Abby Green

DIAMOND IN THE ROUGH
Diana Palmer

SECRET BABY, SURPRISE PARENTS
Liz Fielding

THE REBEL KING
Melissa James

NINE-TO-FIVE BRIDE
Jennie Adams

0809 Rom LP

MILLS & BOON PUBLISH EIGHT LARGE PRINT TITLES A MONTH. THESE ARE THE EIGHT TITLES FOR SEPTEMBER 2009.

THE SICILIAN BOSS'S MISTRESS
Penny Jordan

PREGNANT WITH THE BILLIONAIRE'S BABY
Carole Mortimer

THE VENADICCI MARRIAGE VENGEANCE
Melanie Milburne

THE RUTHLESS BILLIONAIRE'S VIRGIN
Susan Stephens

ITALIAN TYCOON, SECRET SON
Lucy Gordon

ADOPTED: FAMILY IN A MILLION
Barbara McMahon

THE BILLIONAIRE'S BABY
Nicola Marsh

BLIND-DATE BABY
Fiona Harper